PHANTOM LAND
Majestic Files 3

ANDY BRIGGS

TANGLEBOX
BOOKS

PHANTOM LAND

Copyright © 2021 by Andy Briggs

Cover art: Shutterstock

www.andybriggsbooks.com
Twitter: @abriggswriter
Instagram: @itsandybriggs

PHANTOM LAND

nightmares can't be caged

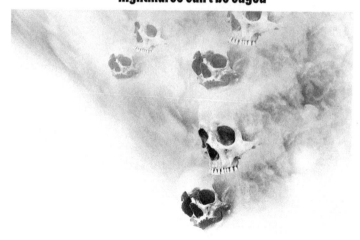

Chapter 1

"Keep quiet and keep down. As if your life depends on it. Because it does."

Tobias Elwood was a hulk of a man, towering six four with biceps that were the girth of his neck. He threw his colossal frame against the front wheel of the Escalade he'd been driving moments before and curled up to conceal himself from view. He grit his teeth to stop them from chattering. Wiping a strand of damp black hair from his sweaty brow, he tilted his head against the fender, allowing the camera to catch his profile *just so*, in a move he'd rehearsed hundreds of times.

"Listen," he hissed, raising a warning finger dramatically. He raised the chunky barrel of his Vaporizer rifle into shot, inches from his cheek as he'd seen countless movie stars do, figuring he'd look just as cool.

Elwood was a natural in front of the lens. He'd sprung to fame by hosting his own regular survival show for five years on the same network. While the cameras rolled, he'd eaten termites, worms and elephant shit, but he did so safe in the knowledge a good night's bed – and a full gourmet dinner - awaited him at the end of every grueling day. Viewers would see him camping under the stars, but Elwood had had enough of that during his time in the Marines. Besides, the crew's union would throw a barrage of lawsuits at his production company if they really had to endure such extremes. It was better for everybody to submit to the power of editing and five-star room service.

But this new show was something different. Something that constantly pushed him and his team to the edge – on and off camera. They faced genuine risks, but the rewards had been beyond anything Elwood had ever dreamed.

Niles Young, the cameraman who had been with him on this new series since the fatal accident in season one, episode two, crouched two yards away, never taking the lens off the star. His boom op cowered close behind. She was confident, but still unused to the waves of fear that were inevitably generated during such encounters. She's also seen footage of what had happened to the last boom… that still sent chills down Niles's spine. Despite Niles's experience in the field, he couldn't hide the naked terror he was feeling. A quick pan to the five other members of Elwood's crew, all hunkered down behind vehicles parked in the street, showed they were on edge too, although disguising it better than he ever could. They clutched a variety of weapons – some also as big as Niles himself.

"Hey!" hissed Elwood. He pointed two fingers at the camera, then at himself. A clear instruction that the action should be on him. He sucked in a breath, then addressed the camera directly. "For three days we've been tracking this thing from town-to-town. But we've always been a step behind. Listening to locals' stories and seeing the prey left in its wake. I tell ya," he gazed in the middle distance. Part act;

part recollection. "This is like nothing we've ever seen before. It's totally new. It exhibits behavior…" he shook his head. It looked as if their task overwhelmed him. He was, but he'd also forgotten his lines. He'd delivered the very same scripted lines smoothly in the car on the way here, and at a rest stop so the best one could be weaved into the final edit. He quickly covered up the blunder as he shifted position. "And now we're here, on the outskirts of Faiyum. It's a completely unimpressive city, about a hundred klicks from Cairo. We've had several credible reports that it has been sighted—"

The swelling noise of barking dogs caused him to twitch his head. The pack's voice rose in numbers as they became increasingly agitated.

Elwood glanced at the camera and smacked his lips. "You can taste it in the air. Like iron. It's close. It's feeding on fear."

Taylor, one of the professional hunters closest to them, held up a small device in her hand, no bigger than a cell phone. "EP's spiking! Confirmed! We have an apport!"

Elwood's jaw muscles worked overtime as he fought his rising unease. He thumbed the safety off his weapon and cocked back the primer. He'd got a lot better at this job in the last eighteen months. In the early days, he'd vomit on camera and had pissed himself once. In one infamous incident, he'd shat his pants. Literally. That had been a difficult episode to edit.

But this prize was the granddaddy. Those others could never come close to what they were hunting now. The number of waivers the network had forced them all to sign should have warned them just how deadly things could get.

"Envelope's peaking," said Taylor in a low voice that carried in the still midnight air. "It's coming this way."

Elwood craned sideways to peek over the hood of the vehicle. His body was coiled, ready to spring forward. Niles angled the camera, knowing that by keeping the star in shot, he was leaving himself exposed. He comforted himself that at least *it* would have to get through Elwood first.

The pitter of claws on concrete came from a dark alley. Rising in volume.

Niles felt the hairs on his arm and the back of his neck prickle. They all did. Such was the nature of the approaching monstrosity.

Then a flurry of fur burst from the alley.

Elwood was on his feet, swinging his vapo around – and scraping the Escalade's paintwork in doing so. His finger itched the trigger as a huge dog burst into the lights of their vehicles. Its fur was wild and unkempt, the slobbering jagged teeth would be enough to make the most hardened animal lover pause from petting it. Yet the flattened ears gave a distinct indication of the terror it felt. Elwood angled his weapon aside. He had no wish of blowing the mutt up on camera. Eight other feral canines sprinted from the alley in a chorus of terrified whimpers. They fled past the team, seeking the sanctuary of the darkness ahead.

Every weapon re-trained back to the alley.

The receding sound of fleeing dogs gave way to a profound silence that was absorbed by the surrounding desert.

Then the headlights flickered. The random interference pattern increased as they slowly faded to half their strength. Niles held his breath. He knew the science, yet science still could not compensate for the emotional responses that had been hard-wired into the human psyche since the dawn of evolution. On cue, the temperature plummeted.

The forty-one degrees went south so quickly that

condensation formed on the vehicles' windshields, and everybody could see their wispy breaths.

It took every neuron of Niles' self-control to battle the *fight-or-flight* response nagging at him to drop the camera and run.

Elwood adjusted his cheek mic and lowered his voice to a mere whisper. "Weapons hot, people. Target approaching."

The darkness in the alley took on a deeper hue, becoming molasses-like as their target drew nearer...

But nothing came.

Elwood frowned and bravely, or insanely, he broke from the cover of the escalade and stepped closer to the mouth of the alley. Niles wanted to yell at him to get back behind cover; that Elwood didn't have to risk his life any further for a good shot, but his throat was dry.

Then it came.

A scream from behind. Elwood whirled around. Niles was quicker with the camera. By the time he adjusted the focus, a Toyota pickup truck had almost completed a three-sixty flip in the air towards him. It came down short – the hood, smashing into the road with a wrenching sound of metal and breaking glass.

Beyond it, a wall of impenetrable darkness was the backdrop to one of the crew who was being hoisted a full fifteen feet in the air – arms and legs flailing as he was drawn towards a pair of blazing red lupine eyes. His screams drowned by a chilling howl that issued from a blood red maw, lined with curved incisors, that appeared from the darkness.

Then all hell literally broke loose.

The Breakthrough

It was a discovery at CERN's Large Hadron Collider in Europe that had first tipped scientists off. While tracking the decay of elusive B mesons, the sub-detectors picked up skewed results. *A violation between lepton flavor universality.* The nonsensical headline failed to make international headlines, but in the world of quantum physics, it was universe-shattering news. The two beauty quarks – b and anti-b quarks flavors for those in the know – occurred with predicable probability.

But not this time.

There was a substantial deviation from the data. Now they knew what to look at, the team repeated the experiment and got the same results. The particles were interacting with a previously unseen force. It proved that the bedrock of physics, the Standard Model, was inaccurate. They had found a new force acting on our world.

A force from a different dimension.

That was the layman's headline the world needed. The Satori Institute in Japan began piling money into research.

The private company appeared to have bottomless pockets as they probed the data and finally announced they had discovered a parallel universe to our own. This wasn't an obscure theoretical discovery; it was a whole new world.

And a whole new form of life existed beyond.

The Institute's work fell silent for several years. The headlines vanished, and the real world focused back on easier to identify problems such as environmental damage, inequality, starvation, disease, and war.

But the Satori Institute hadn't been idle. The discovery of the parallel world brought with it huge questions concerning defense and commerce – what was the threat and what resources could be plundered? Their first major discovery was the life forms that dwelt within. Labeled pandimensional organisms, they widely became known as panspecies, or more simply, *pans*. They were wild creatures of varying intelligence, which all had one thing in common. They were no strangers to our world. They regularly traveled to our dimension and had done throughout history.

Humanity had called them ghosts, spirits, phantoms.

They were all living, breathing creatures. Admittedly, not alive quite in the same way science had looked at life before. Research revealed a huge and complex ecosystem in the *otherworld*. It was one with similar problems to our own, as their environment had stalled. It was no fault of theirs but, as usual, humanity's. It turned out that human's toxic overspill and environmental poisoning wasn't confined to just our dimension. As a result, they were coming over here more than ever to hunt for scarce resources.

Given the right circumstances, the pans could shift the 'vibration' of their atoms and slip into our dimension. A quick change of tune, and they would pop back to their own. At least that's how it was painted for the public. The quantum mechanics string theory behind it all left most people glassy-eyed and baffled. In the end, the term *'apporting'* was used, and that seemed to explain it all.

But they were here and always had been. *Vibrating* at a frequency just enough to slip from view, or phase through walls. The telltale side effect of such transitions was *ectoplasm*, a slimy residue secreted as they fluxed between dimensions. It also meant that the creatures were free from physical harm in our world. Striking them, or even shooting them, was like attacking jello. Even if they could be splattered, the ectoplasm would reform the creatures.

They came in all shapes and sizes. All of which fitted the classic tales of folklore and legend. From the Bogeyman in the closet, to the ghostly phantom haunting a churchyard. They were not the spirits of the dead. Grandma was not haunting the basement. They were cunning animals. Predators.

Further research showed some fed on fresh flesh and bone, like specters, while wights and ghouls settled for a more decayed vintage, so prowled graveyards. However, a majority of pan-species had a more sophisticated diet. They essentially consumed hormones, particularly ones discharged when the victim was *frightened*. It turned out fear was not only tangible, but nutritious too. Pans, particularly the genus branded *phantoms*, could generate pulses of energy that triggered human synapses. A base form of telepathy that simulated the fear response in its prey. In return, humans pumped out quantities of adrenaline and cortisol which the phantoms sensed and fed upon in ways scientists were still trying to understand.

As more species were discovered, their ties with human culture over the millennia became increasingly apparent. The two worlds had evolved in lockstep with one another, with humanity blinded by its own arrogance in thinking that they were at the top of the food chain.

The pans' behavior revealed that they were attracted to large settlements. The growth of sprawling cities was an obvious lure, but it brought with it its own problems. Electromagnetic waves from modern technology deterred them. They would avoid phasing through walls that contained power lines – so seeing a ghostly hand emerge from a light switch or television was unlikely. For the terrified, hiding near your home's powerful router provided a certain amount of shielding from a phantom. Because of this, the phantoms and their ilk preferred old homes, castles, or abandoned buildings. *Exactly* the sort of spooky places they've always been found in.

But as hunger increased, the pans were forced into such environments. This led to the development of military hardware to combat the threat. Electric guns, nicknamed vaporizers, issued a positive stream of super-heated ions. This electrical pulse had the potential to blow a hole in the wall, but all it did to a phantom was *stun* it. The charge solidified the ectoplasm, turning the creature into flesh and blood as we knew it. *Then* it could be bludgeoned into a pool of ectoplasm and killed.

Almost.

The ectoplasm had a memory and would slowly reform the creature. However, all it took was the gunk to be sluiced away with good old H_2O and the animal was literally diluted from existence. Not that it worked on all pans. Specters were immune from such things, but could be stunned in electrified nets, dubbed Tesla nets. Others could be similarly hobbled with exceptionally high-voltage tasers that would fry a human, but merely stun a Bogeyman.

As the weaponry developed, so did the methods of

containing the beasts. The Satori Institute developed translucent plasma screens, trademarked as Tesla Shields, which stopped any pan from phasing through. It also disrupted their ability to apport, meaning once imprisoned, they couldn't simply vanish back into their own dimension.

The science was in place. The hardware was developed, yet the struggle remained to pass a human *into* their dimension so they could begin mining their resources. Instead, pans continued to cross into our world as they had done for millennia.

The standard model of physics was shattered and needed rewriting. Ancient and unique life forms had been discovered, imprisoned, killed, dissected and studied. All the Institute needed now was an idea to make all that research pay off in the most profitable way…

Chapter 2

"Come on, guys!"

Lisa darted from the kitchen and into the lounge, searching for her bag. She didn't think the house was big enough to lose anything, yet items still ended up in the wrong place with alarming frequency. And that included her kids who were sitting in front of the TV, lukewarm pop-tarts halfway to their mouths.

Never had she imagined that at thirty-four she would have been saddled with two children. No, saddled was too harsh a phrase, although it felt like it right now. Sean was a spunky twelve-year-old who was the image of his father... wherever that bastard was right now. Cancun, she last heard, or some other tropical location from which maintenance payments couldn't be enforced. Sean's blue eyes were alight with fascination, which was his standard expression. The kid was a magnet for facts. Nothing could survive his microscopic intrigue. It wasn't enough to want to know how things worked; he wanted to know *why*. Lisa was vaguely aware she once held such a passion for knowledge. But that was back when engineering had been her major, and the possibility of seeing the wonders of the world was just within reach.

Then she turned twenty-two, and every ambition and desire had been snatched from her.

"Emma!" She was barely a year younger than Sean and looked like twins, although she was quieter, but always silently questioning and judging with her big blue eyes. And when she spoke, it was with a brevity and seriousness that made Lisa question if she was on the spectrum. She was far too mature for a child. She was also, it seemed, deaf to her own name. "Emma! You're sitting on my bag!"

The worn leather pouch was poking from under her backside. Lisa slipped it out like a conjuring trick, and the girl remained motionless, her eyes on the screen. Lisa knew without looking what they were watching. The irritating catchy techno-infused Jamaican backbeat theme told her it was their new obsession.

On-screen, handheld camerawork struggled to keep the rather attractive sweating hulk of Tobias Elwood in frame as he sprinted down a dark street, a cartoonishly large rifle in both hands.

"This is it," he growled at the camera. "The big one! All wrapped up for park – the only place in the world you'll be able to see it. And live!"

Sean glanced at his mother, jaw hanging. "He really got it!"

"Uh-huh." Lisa had already tuned out as she stuffed her tablet into the pad, then patted her pockets for her phone. "Where the hell…?"

"Can we go see it?"

The phone was on the table next to her car keys. "Mmm? What?"

"The new exhibit!"

"Um… maybe. What is it?"

Emma regarded her with shock and pointed at the screen. "Weren't you watching?"

"No. Mommy was trying to get ready and not be fired today."

"We *need* to see it," wailed Sean in an overly dramatic voice.

The commercial continued rattling on as Lisa searched for the remote. She listened with half an ear.

"*Exclusively at Phantom Land!*" intoned the narrator. The image switched back to Elwood, strolling down in artificial streets of the theme park. "*Join me here and witness the unveiling of our most terrifying exhibit, this Halloween!*"

"*Then watch the stunning capture, only on Spook Hunters—*" blared the narrator just as Lisa switched it off.

Sean jumped to his feet in astonishment. "Mom! What have you done?"

"I'm late, kiddo!" Lisa kept her voice light, despite the crushing stress weighing on her. Years of improvised parenting had taught her losing her temper always had the opposite effect on her children. They were hard-wired to be stubborn. They got that from her. "I have to get you to school before I go to a very important meeting. Which, if I screw up, means you will never eat again."

"But he was telling us about the unveiling! That's tomorrow night. Can we go?"

"I thought you wanted to go trick-or-treating?"

"We did," Sean said sullenly. "And you said you didn't have time to take us."

"We can go alone," Emma suggested.

"Over my dead body. And yours if you did that," Lisa snapped.

Sean grabbed his bag from the table. "You never have time to do anything we like."

"That's not true…"

"I wish dad was here," he muttered.

Emma was wise enough not to say anything, but she nodded in solidarity.

Lisa knew it was a tantrum designed to tug her heart-strings and make her cave in. Instead, it had the opposite effect, and she couldn't hold back her temper.

"Well, your father isn't here because he cares even less than I do, apparently. And since I'm woefully unappreciated here, what's say we cancel Halloween, anyway?"

"You already did."

She hated that Sean was so accomplished at sniping back. Another trait he had learned from her.

"Do you know how much park tickets are? They're extortionate. And these midnight events are like gold dust." Only last year she had the misfortune of not getting Sean the latest Phantom Land Christmas Lego set before they had sold out, complete with a Tobias Elwood action figure. She had scoured the internet only to find scalpers selling them at triple the price. Scoring hard drugs would have been cheaper. Sean had been heartbroken, and she felt a tsunami of guilt afterwards. She was determined not to feel that, or anything, again. "We can't afford it unless I sell a kidney or something."

"You can sell a kidney?" Emma asked brightly.

Lisa felt a chill. Emma was a little too enthusiastic. Even being stuck in elementary school all day wasn't an obstruction to her finding out how to do it. She only hoped she hadn't given birth to either a serial killer or the second coming. And the way the world was shaping up recently, she couldn't discount either.

Wes Talasky stared at his reflection in the mirror.

He slapped himself on the left cheek. Hard enough to leave a faint red mark, but not enough to hurt too much.

"This is a new day, Talasky. You're running at peak performance."

The doubt on his face made him slap himself again. He drew in a deep breath and studied his reflection.

His short, mousey damp hair stood at all angles, and his cheeks were a little sallow. Not from illness, but an over-abundance of exercise from the new job and an experimental vegetarian regime which he loathed more each day. He had to admit that shaving off the poor excuse of a mustache had been a smart idea. He now looked his age. More or less. Thirty-six years of wiry unfocused flesh who had unspectacularly pinballed through life.

For several years, he'd built an impressive list of companies where he had categorically failed to gain promotion and had eventually left each with no further advancement. In one case, he had exited two positions below where he had first started. His last position at Disney's Animal Kingdom in Florida had been the one he'd hope to keep. And he was down to the last two candidates. As usual, he was the least qualified and let go. Least qualified on paper, maybe, but even as he was shown the door, his ex-employers lavished praise on his work ethics and enthusiasm. Qualities that Wes realized were utterly useless.

After a few weeks of applying for a slate of jobs, and

desperately trying to avoid calling his parents and pleading for a couch to sleep on, he had finally traded Florida's intolerable humidity for the lung-searing dry heat of Las Vegas.

A new start. Although for the last fourteen months it had seemed just like every other misfire in his life and the reality of being broke, single and living in Vegas was gnawing away at his usual bulletproof good cheer.

He pulled his khaki overalls over his torso. The embroidered Phantom Land logo, the park's cute ghostly mascot, Phamo, flashing a thumbs-up, was starting not to look as cool as it once had. A quick look at his cheap plastic Casio digital watch showed him it was time for his appointment.

Shoving aside stacks of folklore books, old supernatural journals and freshly published science papers, from MIT to Russia, detailing the newly minted quantum physics behind pan-dimensional entities, he found his car keys on top of a new *Spook Busters* book. Elwood's grinning face peered from a cover marred by a Sharpie:

To West – keep dreaming – Elwood.

Wes's entire plan of being recruited to Elwood's hunting team had been repeatedly cut down in a flourish of Sharpie ink. He couldn't even get his name right.

Still, Wes hadn't given up. Landing a position as a junior hunter for the park had become his dream.

"Morning, Mister Talasky!"

Wes looked up from the second attempt at unlocking his car. The key needed to be inserted into the Honda's lock *just so* before it turned. Sean was waving at him as he and Emma clambered into the backseat of their Rav4.

"Hi guys." Wes didn't have to leave for work until after two. He'd arrived home at four thirty in the morning, just enough time to grab a few hours' sleep before his perfectly timed run-in on the driveway.

He knew pretending to go to work was a sad excuse to see Lisa, but other than a visit to the grocery store before his shift, she was the highlight of his day. If he hadn't been so calculating, then their working schedules meant they'd never run into one another.

"Have you seen it?" Sean asked breathlessly.

Wes knew he meant the new exhibit, one that had been locked away from all but the most essential staff.

"Sure have," he teased, trying to hold back a yawn.

Emma leaned across the back seat. "What's it like?"

"I can't really tell you… but it's amazing! Oh, hey, I got this." He fished into his backpack and pulled out an Elwood action figure, still in its plastic wrap. He stepped across the drive divider and handed it to Sean.

"Wow! This is brand new!" He held it up to examine the detailing. It even vaguely looked like Elwood. A whole assembly of weapons was tied against the branded backing board. "And with the new vapo!"

"The figures aren't launched until the unveiling tomorrow, so you didn't get it from me." He winked at Sean, and then watched as Lisa stepped from the house and locked the door. Her blonde hair was in a hurried ponytail, swaying like a seductive serpent. He didn't notice the lack of sleep or the stress etching her face. He saw the angel who lived next door.

He only became aware she had spoken when she threw him a quizzical look.

"What?"

"I said 'hey'." Her eyes flicked to the action figure. "And thank you. You shouldn't…"

Wes waved his hand dismissively. "No problem."

"Mom, I didn't clean my teeth!" snapped Emma as she slid back into her seat.

"Lick 'em clean on the way. Hustle people. You don't want mommy fired, do you? Buckle up."

Sean leaned back in his seat, slowly pulling his seatbelt on with one hand, and holding up the action figure with the other. "You get to work with him every day?"

Wes casually shrugged. "What can I say? The guy needs me."

Lisa flashed a supernova smile. "You must be a heck of an expert."

Since childhood, Wes had one guiding principle drummed into him. Honesty. Although, in this situation circumstance decreed he be flexible.

"I know everything about our exhibits. Believe me, Phantom Land couldn't operate without me."

Taking the fifteen south out of Vegas was relatively quiet in the afternoon, as most people were hurrying northbound into the city or had left already. Other than Los Angeles two-hundred sixty miles south, there was little but rock and stones... and the country's, indeed the world's, most visited attraction: Phantom Land.

Located ten miles out of the city, at the toe of Red Rock Canyon National Conservation Area, the forty square miles of dirt had been revolutionized into the world's first supernatural theme park and had since attracted scientific attention from around the globe, and rejuvenated Vegas' reputation as *the* place to be.

By the time Wes had reached the gates, he'd already heard the park's latest Halloween radio jingle three times. The marketing department was in overdrive. Not that they needed to be.

"Phantom Land, the very latest jewel in Vegas' crown! Experience the fright of your life! Dare you enter the banshee caves—" a sudden rush of terrified screams filled the airwaves, but then dissolved into relieved laughter. *"Or take a walk down Apparition Alley – or dare enter the Very Haunted Mansion! Experience your nightmares like never before! And this Halloween, join us for an exclusive event as we unveil our latest star exhibit, captured by the legendary Tobias Elwood. Phantom Land - 100% thrills; 100% chills - and 100% real! Come and face your darkest fears now!"*

Wes took the back road to the parking lot. He stopped at the booth flanked either side by a fifteen-foot-tall crenelated stone wall, designed to resemble a medieval European keep. The quasi-fantasy design ethos was jarred by three-foot metal spheres, mounted on sturdy poles some eight feet tall: Tesla towers lined the entire circumference, each twenty yards apart. When activated, they formed the SkyShield and draped the entire site in an electromagnetic cloak to keep the exhibits firmly inside.

The guard double-checked his ID, despite them being on speaking terms for the last six months. Wes drove in and found his allocated spot in the Bogeyman lot, furthest from the pedestrian entrance gate. The trams ferrying passengers from the parking lots only ran during operating hours, so it took him five minutes before he walked past Elwood's gleaming Porsche Boxster parked feet away from the gate.

Wes girded himself for another overly long shift.

Chapter 3

Howard Clarkson was, by nature, a complete bastard. His single-minded conservative attitude promoted his own welfare over everybody else's. It had led to Dynamic Solutions being one of the West Coast's fastest growing marketing agencies. With over three-hundred million dollars in turnover, they had harvested clients from Google, Apple and Huawei, with a growing cluster of tech companies across Silicon Valley. They were emerging fast, ready to take on the biggest players as more clients clamored for that little Clarkson magic.

The latest coup had been to hook the attention of *Mofa Quantum*, a pioneering Chinese company on the cusp of launching the world's first qubit phone. Clarkson had been to Shanghai several times to woo the CEO. It wasn't a huge company, but it was entrepreneurial, and their device was poised to revolutionize the mobile phone market. It would make Steve Jobs announcement of the iPhone look like amateur hour.

That's if both Mofa Quantum and Dynamic Solutions could get it right.

It was a risky venture, but Clarkson had made his fortune in the casinos on the Golden Strip and thrived on risk… and a good deal of research. In the case of making his fortune, it had involved counting cards. Mofa Quantum may well be a small outfit, and the marketing deal would require a little *quid pro quo*, but the potential reeked of billion-dollar possibilities. Four months of serenading their President and traveling between Vegas and Shanghai had finally netted them the contract. Almost. The company's President's imminent arrival was surely to sign the deal.

Which is why looking at the array of *tat* on the desk in front of him was giving him chest pains.

"You're gonna sink the entire deal because of *gift bags*?" He spat the words like a foul taste.

Lisa Mammott still hadn't sat down from the moment she had revealed the hastily assembled array of gadgets, gathered from the very best Silicon Valley start-ups that owed her favors.

Clarkson picked up a pair of augmented reality glasses, no larger than a pair of bulky shades, and inspected them with disdain.

"The Chinese love their tech," Lisa said defensively, "and those glasses are not even on the market yet. They're revolutionary AR–"

Clarkson dropped them with a clunk that indicated something delicate had broken.

"They were probably manufactured over in China. Or worse, Japan. Mofa is an industry leader and we're offering them other people's crap?"

"I didn't think a bunch of chips from the Bellagio would be enough."

Clarkson narrowed his eyes. He had hired Lisa because she was good at her job, a highly talented business liaison with a great record in tech companies. And also because she was hot, and he liked to keep the business looking pretty. After all, they were in the image game. Not something he could openly admit in this draconian era, where every little joke was seen as harassment.

"It would be better than this bag of turds you've presented me with." He paced the room, sucking in lungfuls of air and windmilling his arms. His joints clicked with every revolution. "Jesus Christ, Lisa. Are you trying to kill me?" He looked out of the window. It gave him a line of sight to the Bellagio Hotel's fountain display. Columns of water shot into the air, synchronized to music for no more reason than to impress the passing crowds. It was that over the top showmanship that had drawn him to Vegas to begin with. "The President of Mofa is probably in the air already! This deal will put afterburners on my company. Everything has to look good. Everything!"

"You gave me less than two days' notice!"

Clarkson whirled around and slammed his palm on the desk, making her jump. "Oh, so this is *my* fault? How about this, do better, or you're fired."

Lisa tried to speak twice before the words came out. "You're going to fire me over a gift bag?"

"Yes." He stared at her. He knew, just like a dozen other people this week, that she wanted to call him a bastard. He could read it in her eyes, and her lips were pushed together to form the words... but she regained control. He was slightly annoyed that she didn't have the guts. Then again, if she had, then he'd have to fire her in a public display of humility to keep the other employees on edge. Then who would help him out with his current problem? He forced himself to calm down.

"An attitude like that is going to get you nowhere." He enjoyed her twitch of anger. "Chinese culture is a very sensitive one. Gifts are integral in laying the path of future relations. What message will this send them?"

Lisa tactfully remained silent.

"Understand, Lisa, this is potentially a bigger client than Apple. They're the seed of an apple right now. A seed that is going to grow into a giant fucking Redwood."

Lisa bit her bottom lip, desperate not to correct his tangled analogy.

"When they arrive tomorrow, they expect to be blown away. The shit they showed me in Shanghai is unbelievable. *That's* what I need from this." He flicked the silk gift bag off the table. "It needs to convince them that, while they can do the amazing, *we* can do the impossible."

The grating of the shovel across concrete used to set Wes' teeth on edge, but now he was so inured to it he barely noticed. The thick, clear gelatinous mass on the floor had the consistency of molasses, and he had to patiently wait for it to ooze from the shovel into the wheelbarrow.

"You guys went and got yourself all riled up last night, huh?" He glanced at the opaque wall at the rear of the pen. It was a sliding energy screen that held the exhibits safely back during scheduled maintenance. He swapped the shovel for a damp mop and half-heartedly ran it over the concrete floor. The gunk popped and sizzled as the water washed it away. "You've got to seriously reconsider your bioplasm excretions. It's disgusting."

"Hey, Wes!"

The electric buzz of the open-sided Metro tram was no louder than a whisper, despite pulling the four carriages, all one hundred seats empty. Kirk Freeman was at the wheel, possibly the most enthusiastic *spookologist* in the whole park, and with the boyish looks of a young Johnny Depp, supposedly, he doubled his income through tips alone. Kirk drew alongside and popped open a Pepsi.

"Poltergeist giving you more grief again?"

"Ever since our new boy arrived, they've been antsy and having ectoplasm parties every night." Wes threw the shovel, mop, and bucket into the wheelbarrow and rolled it out of the enclosure. His gaze flickered to the large building at the center of the park. Its peak was just visible above the ornate topiary.

The Enclave.

The scaffolding had only been cleared a few days ago, revealing the sharp black obsidian pyramid gleaming in the sun.

"I know how they feel. Just driving past that thing, you can feel it. Even with the Raudive insulation." He guzzled back half the can before offering it to Wes, who declined with a shake of the head. "I've had to do a couple of dummy tours through there. It's horrible. You can hear a voice right here." He tapped the top of his head. "Y'know, like when you hear white noise and swear there's a voice in it?"

Wes pulled the enclosure door shut. It was made from tempered glass, laced with a fine mesh that circulated a constant current that stopped the poltergeist from escaping. He touched his key card against a recessed scanner. The security was reactivated. With a hiss, the mechanical lock snapped into place. An LED changed from red to green and, a few seconds later, the rear Tesla screen deactivated, freeing the poltergeist into the wider enclosure.

Not that they could see the invisible creatures directly.

The windows tinged red as the current flowed. It brought the dark shapes into view. Poltergeist. These had been caught in a Bavarian hotel where they had been causing hell on the poor staff and guests. They resembled amorphous blobs that size of beach balls, with spindly appendages that served as arms. Other than that, they didn't have any obviously recognizable features such as eyes or mouths. Their natural calls sounded like mischievous children laughing. Centuries of evolution had ensured that it sent shivers down even the most hardened person's spine, allowing the pans to feed from the generated fear. The Bavarians immediately got to work hurling the objects inside their enclosure – balls, teddy bears and an assortment of toys. Already they were agitated to such a frenzy that rivulets of ectoplasm splashed against the glass.

"They're hungry," Kirk pointed out.

"We'll keep them hungry a little longer," said Wes, glancing at his Casio. It was an hour before sunset. "We're opening in fifteen minutes."

The night-time hours suited the park's ecosystem and fit perfectly into the rhythm of Vegas. People could still catch a show before descending into their nightmares. He lifted the barrow and walked back towards the maintenance hut.

Kirk drove alongside. "Any more news on your application?" He had followed Wes' lack of career progress with interest. Not because he had any desire to be promoted from his current position – he always said that it landed him far too many hot girls to ever want to move on. Wes believed him too. Several times he had caught Kirk fooling around in the bushes with a guest who had just started to 'feel faint'. Kirk made the perfect dashing hero coming to the rescue.

"Calvin said I'd hear before we open the exhibit."

"Tomorrow?"

"I hope so." He felt an unusual surge of optimism. "I know I aced the theory test. And I heard they were desperate to fill four positions on this cycle. This is my moment."

By the time Wes stowed the cleaning gear and returned to the admin block, the gates were open and thousands of tourists, all desperate to be terrified, had flooded into the park. At 4am's closing time, almost sixty thousand people would have been scared shitless.

He diligently took a shower, ensuring any residual ectoplasm was washed off, as per the security routines to prevent any contamination from leaving the park, then he dressed, ready for his break. Before he could get anywhere near the refectory, Calvin Tarsov stepped from his office, waving his tablet.

"Talasky! You never responded to the roster!" His supervisor's thick Russian accent made him sound pissed off, even when he was in a good mood. Which he seldom was.

Wes took out his phone. The entire park operated around a sophisticated virtual hub. The problem was one of bandwidth. As the park expanded and the data load exponentially increased, it meant the system often got jammed. Sure enough, there was a flashing notification on his roster app that he'd missed in the shower.

"I've only just got this–"

"And you were ten minutes late!"

"I was fifteen minutes early!"

Calvin tapped his tablet. "Not according to this."

"Check at the gate—"

"I don't want excuses, Talasky! The system works even if you do not!"

He would say that, Wes fumed. He was a proponent of installing the work management system when the park was being built. Rumor suggested it was his uncle's security firm in Moscow that had won the lucrative contract, but had been unable to deliver. Ever since, they had been playing catch-up.

"And now you're supposed to be covering the Banshee Tunnel."

"It's my break—"

"Suzanne is sick again. Something about bleeding from the ears."

Another industrial accident, Wes thought glumly. There had been a few of them lately. All quickly covered up, of course.

"I'll go after my break."

"You go now."

Argument was futile. Wes sucked in his bitter reply and simply nodded. Maintaining Calvin's good side, or less hostile one, was critical to any chance he had of progressing out of maintenance. He turned, but Calvin hadn't finished with him.

"And you just lost a week's vacation time."

"What?"

"You know the rules. You must use your vacation time up in twelve months."

"How am I supposed to know that? For the first six months, I didn't have any. And now you're saying I've lost it? I'll take it next week."

"Too late. You lose. It gone!" He snapped his fingers.

"I'm being punished for *coming* to work?"

Calvin gave a slight shrug. "I only enforce rules. At least there is a good side to all of this." Wes looked at him hopefully. "You now get another three weeks. Use them wisely this time. Oh, it means that your perks package is reset."

The 'perks' amounted to two free entrance tickets, a fifty-dollar gift card that could be used in the gift shops and restaurants, and a baseball cap with the park's logo on it.

"I'm so happy." Wes spun on his heels and marched back down the corridor before he said something he'd regret. He caught sight of Calvin thumping a fat finger on his tablet before he disappeared into his office.

Wes wasn't hungry. The vegetarian lunch he'd bought from the grocery store could wait. He stepped out of the air-conditioned corridor and into the dry heat. The backstage area was cordoned off from the guests, hidden behind faux-cliffs and a dense forest of Joshua trees. The admin block was next to the staff canteen, which was currently sparse, as most of the crew were out amongst the guests. Next to it was a small medical center used primarily for guests who had bumps and scrapes. Further beyond was the park's own fire service and one of several sub-stations providing for the power thirsty site.

The squat command hub lay just beyond. It was the operational heart of Phantom Land. The architect's original plans had rendered all kinds of exotic structures – from a multi-facetted glass hub resembling a fly's eye, to a giant multi-legged saucer, reminiscent of LAX's Theme Building. In the end, it was decided that flamboyant architecture was a complete waste of money for a building that nobody would see. Instead, the command hub became a bland white concrete structure that looked like a rejected military bunker.

In the parking area outside it, amongst the handful of gas-powered jeeps used primarily outside the park, was a train of parade floats, all artfully designed to reflect folklore from around the world. They were lined up ready for the first show of the evening. Dozens of the park's *cast*, the actors who couldn't get work elsewhere, were dressed as various ghostly entities. They limbered up for their dance routine, which would take them a full thirty minutes to circle even a small section of the park.

Taking the coveted final position was a huge, armored vehicle painted with the park's livery. It was an Oshkosh L-ATV, built for the Army as a replacement for the Humvee. The park had acquired one and fitted a giant vaporizer on the back. Four good-looking actors, portraying the team from Spook Hunters, climbed into the Oshkosh. The two guys had their shirts partially open, revealing muscular chests. The uniforms for the two girls bulged at the seams.

To be young again, Wes thought. The park was so vast that walking in the heat would exhaust him before he reached the Banshee Tunnels. He took the nearest electric maintenance buggy and drove to the automatic gates that separated the backstage from the park proper. The gate wheeled open, and Wes drove through at barely more than a walking pace.

It wouldn't be sunset for another hour, yet already the streets, avenues, and boulevards were filling out with excited guests. Phantom Land had adopted Halloween as their holy day. There was no sign of decorations, not a pumpkin in sight. As soon as the gates closed at 4am, an army of set decorators would move in and turn it into a unique wonderland, made more special by tomorrow's unveiling of the new phantom.

His phone buzzed with a notification from his app. He pulled to the side. Any phone used while driving in the park was a firing offence. It was an internal email:

YOUR APPLICATION!

Wes paused and looked back at the door he had just exited. Calvin must have sent it straight after entering his office. With a shaking finger, he tapped the screen to read it.

Your application for Junior Hunter has been processed!

The upbeat introduction was swiftly followed by a crushing rejection. Despite the heat, Wes shivered. Calvin hadn't even had the balls to tell him to his face. Worse, it was cheerfully signed off by Elwood with a spikey: *Better luck next time!*

"Son of a bitch," he muttered under his breath.

Elwood's voice seeped into his consciousness. Wes looked up to see the man himself walking towards the back-stage gate, surrounded by a family all seeking autographs and selfies. Elwood posed obligingly, then continued to the gate. Wes impulsively abandoned the cart and caught up with him.

"Hi, Elwood." Wes flicked a limp smile.

Elwood shot him a fleeting look. "Hey…" Wes' name died on his lips, and he didn't slow down. They'd worked together since before the park opened. Pissed, Wes side-stepped to block his path. "My application as junior hunter was knocked back again. Do you remember we talked about it a couple of weeks ago? In the canteen," he added helpfully.

Elwood didn't disguise his irritation as he looked Wes up and down, pulling a name from the furthest reaches of memory. "Right. West… that's right. Hey sorry, them's the breaks. There's always next time."

"Wes. It's *Wes*. And this was the *next time*. The next-next time. We talked about this. You even gave me advice on how to get through."

"Did I? That doesn't sound like me."

Wes was expecting a mumbled half-assed excuse. Instead, Elwood grinned and playfully punched his arm. "Anyway, I meant *next* time." Then, to Wes's astonishment, Elwood snatched Wes' cell phone, flicked the camera on with one hand while the other draped around Wes's neck, pulling him closer. Elwood pushed his tongue out and gave a long "Gggaaaahh!" as he took a selfie. Then, with a wink, he shoved the phone back into Wes's hand and marched through the gate.

Chapter 4

The high-pressure spray made short work of the liquid ectoplasm on the walls, but the more congealed excretions required Wes to work them hard with a long-handled wire brush.

"Stubborn bastards…"

Another blast of the jet dislodged the stubborn mass, and it dropped to the floor, shattering. Wes stopped the spray and took a moment to wipe the sweat from his brow with his forearm. Cleaning the enclosure was hard work, made worse by the heat. Around him the cage was set up as some kind of post-apocalyptic diorama, with rusty swings and fragments of industrial piping. He knew it was supposed to represent the exclusion zone around the Chernobyl reactor where the phantom exhibits had been caught, but the art department had favored a *Mad Max* vibe.

He brushed up the resin-like plasm fragments and dropped them into a bucket of water, which dissolved them with a hiss. Then he turned the pressure jet back on the slime. His mind was racing with a hundred witty retorts he should have fired at Elwood. They had been working together since Wes' first day. They'd been on several team building events, and dozens of social drinks for various people's birthdays, as well as parties for Thanksgiving and Christmas. And still the moron kept getting his name wrong.

This was not how Wes had envisioned his life panning out – cleaning up ghost crap. He stared at a mound of ectoplasm as he blasted it with the power hose, imagining he was tearing off Calvin's stupid grin. He was so absorbed in flights of revenge that he sprayed a semi-congealed puddle of ectoplasm off an overhanging pipe at such an angle it dropped straight on him.

The gloop hit his exposed forearm, and he immediately felt it prickle like a hundred stinging jellyfish massaging his arm.

"BASTARD!" he yelled aloud, turning the jet on his own arm. The high pressure liquid hurt like hell and the pain doubled as the excretion dissolved on his skin, leaving red pimples which continued to throb.

Mocking laughter came from beyond the humming translucent Tesla screen that pinned the display's six phantoms in the corner. Unlike the poltergeist, these Class II phantoms were clearly visible. Suspended pale yellow torsos some three feet long and covered in warty skin. Their long spindly arms ended in four scythe-like fingers that occasionally prodded the Tesla screen. Their heads had a semblance of human characteristics, but it was nothing more than an impression. Their mouths were wide watermelon like smiles, revealing hundreds of jagged fangs.

These guys possessed animal cunning and were predators, capable of severe maiming should they choose to do so. Fortunately, Class IIs were more notorious as pet-eaters. These in question had feasted on the abundant wildlife that reclaimed Chernobyl in the absence of man. One characteristic they adopted from humans was a distinctive hyena-like laughter, which they all bleated on seeing Wes in pain. Pain and fear were something they feasted upon, as well as the occasional tasty stray.

"Think that's funny, do you?" snarled Wes. He'd had enough of his colleagues mocking him; for the exhibits to do so was simply too much. "Laugh this off!"

He turned the spray onto the phantoms. The liquid easily passed through the electromagnetic screen and sent the phantoms howling in every direction as they tried to avoid its stinging blast.

"Who's laughing now?" Wes snarled, only stopping when he noticed a crowd of some seven guests watching him from beyond the perimeter screen, ignoring the 'TEMPORARILY CLOSE FOR MAINTENANCE' sign. They didn't look impressed, particularly one teenage Emo girl who simply blew a chewing gum bubble until it popped, killing Wes's sense of moral superiority with it.

Embarrassed, he hurried from the enclosure and released the Class IIs, who immediately patrolled their territory to check nothing had changed. The crowd ignored Wes as he put the tools back in a plastic storage barrel bolted to the side of the cage. Made from bright yellow plastic, they were emergency caches equipped with a fire extinguisher, a vapo, heavily tinted wrap around augmented reality shades for spotting invisibles, and a carefully folded Tesla net. A green first aid kit was for treating regular wounds. The yellow one had more exotic remedies to deal with the dangers of the various exhibits, including such diverse items such as noise-canceling ear defenders. It was also handy for unofficial stowing of the cleaning products.

Wes used a tube of lotion from the yellow kit. The pale cream was made especially for the park. On one side was the logo, the other listed a string of chemical ingredients. Wes lathered it over his puckered flesh. The blue gel popped as it came into contact with the blemishes on his arm, and he felt the pain ease. It was a minor wound, but he knew from experience that ectoplasm rashes could last for days.

He snapped the cache shut and engaged the electronic lock using his key card, then finished the water in the cooling flask hanging from his belt, next to his flashlight. That was one of the park's golden safety rules. Never find yourself in the dark.

Despite the clear skies, the night-time temperature hadn't dipped, and the heat was sapping his strength more than usual. He put that down to the lack of sleep from his early morning Lisa encounter. He reflected on the sad existence he had carved out for himself. Other than being the handy neighbor, he wasn't a blip in her life. He was the completely interchangeable guy next door, and nothing was going to change that. He didn't have the courage to ask her out, and even if he did, the moment she said no, then he didn't have the money to move either. He glanced at the caged phantoms and was struck by a sense of jealousy. He wasn't intrepid; it was a weakness that had probably denied him the promotion to his dream job. A hunter on Elwood's team. A chance to see the world and research the fascinating creatures. His window to be the next Jane Goodall of the phantom world had slammed shut.

A glance at the roster revealed he was supposed to be in

the aviary five minutes ago, not that he had any motivation to be punctual. Not anymore. Maybe it was time to move on?

He heard Kirk's energetic patter before the whine of the tram as it drew up alongside the Phantom enclosure and began playing a video on the multiple screens hanging from the side of the trailers. It was Elwood giving a pre-recorded lecture on the exhibits. Wes automatically tuned out as he walked to the driver's cab. Kirk was checking messages on his cell as he waited for the loop to play out.

"Hey Wes... wow, cheer up. It may never happen." Wes's expression told him otherwise. "Oh... the promotion?"

"Didn't get it."

"Sorry." He genuinely meant it, too. "You should do this," he nodded to the trailers behind him. "You know everything, and they want to hear it. The questions I get asked. I don't know half the answers."

"I'm not really a people person," Wes mumbled.

"Then what kinda person are you?"

"One who wants a ride to the aviary."

Kirk indicated to the space alongside him. The centrally positioned steering wheel gave plenty of free space on either side. Wes gratefully climbed onboard just as the video came to a halt and the indicator on Kirk's screen told him to drive. The entire operation could easily have been automated, but the park believed that having human contact guiding the visitors through the exotic exhibits was essential hand-holding.

Kirk angled the microphone clinging to his cheek. "Okay folks, you'll see plenty of other phantoms as we continue on, and let me tell you, if those poor old Class IIs gave you the chills, you're gonna be scared out of your pants over what's coming next."

Kirk threaded the tram onto a special lane kept separate from the main walkways around the park, both for safety and efficiency. The through-put of guests on the tram ride was critical, and the park didn't want to see anybody miss out because of slow pedestrians blocking the vehicles.

The electric engine gave nothing more than a slight rise in pitch as they climbed an incline. "Next up we're taking you to Transylvania, and the dark demons that lurk there." He gave a terrific Vincent Price laugh, an impression that was lost on ninety percent of the guests behind him.

Inside the command hub was a bleeding-edge showcase of technology. One side of the room was dedicated to security, with a high-definition floor to ceiling screen that could display every single security camera at once. An AI computer system helped identify problems, meaning the crew needed to monitor the park was minimal.

The other half dealt with the operations. A similar screen showed a map of the park. Data could be overlaid, from power consumption through to the flow of guests. No aspect of the park was overlooked by detailed computer modeling. Every enclosure could be individually singled out for inspection, and every exhibit watched, monitored and tracked. Nothing had been left to chance.

This was the proud domain of Thomas Blake, the park's

senior operations manager. The man who had ultimate authority on the ground. He'd had a distinguished career as a Mission Control Specialist at NASA before being head-hunted for Elon Musk's Space X operation. His operational expertise under extreme pressure had made him an ideal candidate to run the park, and the Satori Institute didn't spare a dime in tempting him. He was a family man whose career had been beyond what he'd dreamed it could be in junior high - spaceships and ghosts. A potent cocktail for any man-child. He often referred to it as *his* park. Nobody had the courage to correct him.

The hub's twelve permanent crew had all been there from the beginning, split between the day and night shifts, keeping the same six players together in a tight family unit. Blake was a pleasant boss, and he liked to keep the atmosphere jovial. Plus, they all knew, just as he did, that the park could be controlled solely by the AI system and his three immediate managers: Ed Tanaka, a Japanese-American Caltech graduate who had landed the position as his first job. Sophie Clarke, a native Kenyan, who had earned her spurs in South Africa running a conservation park. She had impressed Blake during her interview that he'd cut it short and offered her the job there and then. And Hugh Pine, at fifty-eight the eldest on the team and a Brit who had worked at a data analytic company in Cambridge that had the dubious reputation for manipulating social media. He was known as *Mr Data*, and all feared annoying him lest he extracted his revenge digitally. Rumor had it he'd once made his landlord insolvent at a keystroke.

Blake checked the clock on the screen as it turned over to 7 pm. Officially nighttime. "Okay folks, it's snag time. What have we got?"

Tanaka called up the list. "Toilet block C23 is out of

order. Backed up *again*. Our team is at a loss as to why it keeps happening, so an external maintenance crew is looking into it tomorrow. It's like a swamp in there."

"If a broken john is the only problem for the day, that's fine by me. What else?"

"Some issues in the Poltergeist Café. A faulty smoke detector has been going off all afternoon. On Terror Boulevard several streetlights are blowing out because of a surge—"

"Why did we have a surge?"

Sophie swiveled around him her chair and rubbed her eyes, which smarted from far too much screen time. "We had an intermittent generator in the Enclave and switched to back-up while maintenance is taking a look."

With the swipe of his fingers across the pad on his desk, Blake put video feeds of the Enclave up on the enormous screen. Even under the floodlights, the dark pyramid looked ominous. The view continued *through* the wall of the building – a mixture of smart CGI and cleverly placed cameras as they switched to the ones inside. It was a bit too showy for Blake, who preferred simple, robust systems.

Inside, the display team was putting the finishing touches to the walkways around the star exhibit. They wore fluorescent hazmat suits with soundproof helmets that made them look more like astronauts. It was a specially designed kit that filtered out some of the disturbing *emotional* seepage the creature naturally emitted. Such protection gear was mandatory for anybody spending over fifteen minutes in there. The guests wouldn't have such a luxury. Audio dampers positioned around the pyramid interfered with the Raudive voices the exhibit generated. It was a brown noise that infiltrated the brain, tickling the language centers and forming voices from the harsh wash of static. The dampers made things tolerable for the short time they would be in there, but spending any longer could lead to psychological side effects. More research was needed, but the Satori Institute didn't see the need to make it public. There was scaring people, and there was *scaring people*. They were savvy enough to know which one paid.

While transporting the beast from Egypt had seen two men go insane and kill themselves. A third victim, a woman, had attempted to do the same, but had been saved. Physically, at least. Her mental scars may never heal. Large payoffs to the victims' families had helped keep the lid on such matters.

The Tesla shields around the creature were the most advanced the park had produced and were currently pulsing at such a frequency that the camera could only show a monstrous shadow shifting behind the pulsing screen. A giant of a humanoid, some twenty-five feet high. Blake was glad they couldn't make out its features. He'd seen it twice already and regretted both times. While he understood the desire for people to see these freshly uncovered creatures, and appreciated the human need to face fear, he thought the Enclave was pushing it a step too far.

Some things deserved to remain in the shadows.

There were still some things people should fear.

"All safety checksums are green," Sophie continued. "And we are on schedule for the unveiling tomorrow."

"Ah, tomorrow," muttered Blake. Today the park was running at seventy-two percent capacity, solely because many people were hanging back to see the new star. It was Halloween tomorrow. From that point onwards, they'd push almost 100% until February at least.

"I have an amber light on the Specter Corral," Hugh noted.

"Show me."

Blake was relieved when the Enclave image was replaced by a feed of the Specter Corral, designed to look like to sort of Transylvanian village only found in old B-movies. It hugged the curves of the Rabid River that circled the park. The boat ride, on miniature ghost ships, was an attraction itself, but the water provided an additional security barrier. Most pan species hated water and gave it a wide berth.

The specters themselves were barely visible. Tapering, spindly creatures, they usually lurked amongst the scenery until a tram pulled up. Then they would spring out at high-speed and furiously attacked the energy screen. Blake watched as they did just that. The guests were whooping with terrified delight as they taunted the creatures. In return, the specters fed off their fear. But unlike most of the phantoms, specters were ferocious carnivores. The panthers of the pan world. They craved flesh and blood.

Blake shook his head. "Hands, feet, arms, legs and heads inside the car at all times... or they'll get chewed off."

The carnivorous hunters were often found alone in the wild. The designers had made the mistake of placing a dozen of them in a single spacious enclosure. Since then, they had learned to swarm with the deadly efficiency of a shoal of sharks. The researchers had been delighted, desperate to study their new emerging behavior.

Hugh superimposed a gauge showing the Tesla screen's power consumption. The six bars had gone from green to yellow and were still climbing.

"Should I increase the voltage?" his fingers were already hovering over the controls. He was a man of supreme caution.

"Just wait."

Another bar crept up as the swarm looped around and smashed into the protective screen with renewed fury.

"If the breakers kick in–"

"Just wait…"

Ying Yue, the young Chinese-American technician, looked up from her desk. As one of the juniors, she had not yet had a chance to see the exhibits as closely as the senior crew, and her fascination grew each day. Next to her sat David Steinberg, who was the second dog's body. He'd only been there for four months and had just heard that he'd been accepted as a junior hunter on the training program. He was still riding high from the news.

All eyes were on the power gauge as it turned orange. The hub filled with the sound of the taunting guests, the furious spectral wails, and the harsh sizzle of the energy screen.

Then the gauge hit red.

And at that moment, the tram pulled away. The specters decided not to follow it, instead they fled back to the dark nooks and crannies of their enclosure to await the next visitors. The energy bar plummeted back into the yellow.

Blake released a pent-up breath.

"One of these days, I ought to drop the screen on that moron. That would turn a good day into a great day. Who was the spookologist? Was it Kirk?" Hugh nodded. "Tell him I want a word with him at the end of his shift." He took a sip of his lukewarm coffee. "Anything else?"

"Head Office received elevated threats from some animal rights activists. Security wanted to review procedures with you." Tanaka knew what Blake's response would be.

"Not now, please! Schedule something next week. I don't have time. Hey, Ying, can you deal with it?"

"Yes, sir."

"Good. It's going to be a bunch of crazy crusader chatter, so don't take it too seriously." He looked at the next item on his checklist. "Okay everybody, up next: the SkyShield simulation. Complete power outage. I want this to be by the numbers as if it were real."

With so many back-ups, it was inconceivable they would ever reach a Zero Outage scenario, which involved a total loss of power. The ultimate worst-case scenario. With multiple substations, smart power management, and multiple redundancies in the shields, it was deemed more likely the park would be struck by a meteor than all the failsafes dying at the same moment. However, the risk of one or two enclosures going down was *very* real. That's why they needed the SkyShield. It would enclose the park, preventing the spooks from apporting back to their own dimension, or worse, getting out into the wild. There would be just enough time for the crew to capture the escapees and confine them to one of several backup facilities.

The atmosphere in the room became charged as everybody readied themselves. They treated the simulations seriously. It was one of the more enjoyable aspects of Blake's job. Especially when the ground crew were unaware of the practice. Watching them scramble was always worth a laugh. Sadly, not tonight. With guests in the park, it would have to be a virtual run.

He watched on his personal screen as a 3D image of the park highlighted the Tesla coils mounted along the exterior walls. They burst to life, forming an electromagnetic dome across the park. He listened to the team report in, each monitoring the vast amounts of power the system sucked in. As long as the shields around the exhibits held, they could do without luxuries, such as air conditioning and catering.

The virtual dome closed around the park, sealing the

exits for guests and pans alike. The onsite teams would scramble into action to contain the escaped spook, then everything would snap back to the way it had been. It was a serious piece of defense, and one Blake was confident they would never have to use.

Chapter 5

The barking dog could be heard across the dark parking lot, yet few people paid it any heed as they went about their evening grocery shop.

Sarah Dillon shouldered the hardware store door open, arms laden a cardboard carton filled with vital supplies. She took several steps towards her battered open-top jeep before she spotted the dog.

"Oh, no…" she breathed when she saw the Ford pickup twenty yards away. The windows were rolled up and a poor Labrador inside was exhaustedly pawing at the glass. Indignant, she marched across and tried the handle. Locked. The dog was clearly weak and exhausted. How long had it been trapped inside the furnace?

"Whose car is this?" she yelled across the lot. Her dark brown eyes scanned the handful of people around. Nobody responded. "Shit…"

She placed her carton on the floor and fished around until she found what she wanted – a huge lug wrench. She tucked her auburn bangs in her marine style cap and weighed the tool in her hand.

"Back up, buddy." The dog didn't understand and was too exhausted to do anything but sit on the hot leather seat.

Dillon swung the wrench at the tinted rear passenger window. It imploded in a shower of safety glass and the car alarm squealed. Ignoring it, she reached through, feeling the burning air inside, and unlocked the driver's door. She yanked it open and scooped the dog out. The poor animal shivered in her arms and feebly licked her face, but it didn't have the strength to do much more.

"You stupid bitch!" howled a voice of indignation from behind. A brick shithouse of a man in an ill-fitting denim jacket and blue baseball cap looked from his beloved car to her. "What've done to my pickup?"

"This is your dog?"

"Bitch, you're gonna pay for this!" He stepped threateningly forward, so fueled by rage that he failed to register Dillon's lack of fear. She gently placed the dog on the ground and picked up the wrench. "You gotta be off of your skull on—"

In one fluid motion, Dillon sharply stood, using her momentum to swing the wrench in an arc that ended with pinpoint accuracy on the man's jaw. She saw teeth fly as he fell and cracked his head on the floor.

"You should have left the window open! You almost killed this poor doggie."

The man writhed in pain, both hands clutching his fracture jaw.

Dillon dropped the wrench into her carton, picked them both up and stepped over the hillbilly.

"You should be ashamed of yourself, hurting an innocent animal like that." She kicked the man in the stomach, crushing the breath from him, then gave a little click of her tongue. The dog's ears pricked. She indicated to her jeep and walked away. The Labrador obediently followed.

Some people, she thought, are simply not fit for society...

The warehouse was out towards McCarran airport, but not quite close enough to jack up the rental price. Not that Dillon was bothered. They had rented it for a week and would have done so, whatever the cost. It was a handy base camp for their operation.

She parked outside and scooped the carton from the backseat. The Labrador obediently hopped out, energized after she had let it drink from a water bottle. She cast a look around, checking nobody was paying her any attention. There was nobody around; only the sound of a private jet throttling for take-off echoing from the avenue of identical warehouses. She entered.

"Hey guys! I think I've got everything."

An unmarked white van was parked in the center of the hangar, next to a pair of trestle tables. Thirteen people sitting around the table on foldable chairs turned to look at her. At twenty-four, Dillon was the youngest member of the team, but they hadn't known that when they joined the cause. It was her passion that had drawn the others in. Her clarion call on Facebook, WhatsApp and every other social media platform she joined had been persuasive for the few who responded. They had come from all around the world, and from all walks of life: two housewives, one whose name she forgot, the other was Jenna. There was a vet in there, which had excited her before realizing he was the animal variety. Derek was an ex-policeman. There was a mail woman, and several store clerks. She struggled to remember names, but that wasn't important as long as they fulfilled the roles assigned to them. After the operation, they would never see one another again.

A bespectacled hippy almost toppled from his chair when he saw the dog following her.

"Who the hell ordered the mutt?"

Dillon lifted a bowl of chips from the table and tossed them onto a pile of paperwork. She put the bowl down and took a bottle of water amongst the sodas and beers on the table, and filled it. The dog eagerly lapped it up, tail wagging furiously.

"Poor thing was locked in a car, Kyle."

Kyle was thirty. He hadn't asked too many questions, but burned with just as much fervor for their cause as she did.

"We can't take it with us."

"Of course not. But I couldn't leave it there to die." She looked indignantly at him. "What do you take me for?" While it had been her cause, her idea, Kyle had been the real dynamo in bringing the plan together. She glanced around the hangar, noticing everybody was here. "Why're you all back early?"

Kyle waved his cell phone. "I got all the last bits of intel we needed when it opened this evening." He selected a photo and showed her. "The scaffolding is down. It looks all ready to launch tomorrow. Me and Anna had a good scout around." He gestured to a pretty woman with blonde braids and skinny jeans. Dillon tried to ignore a pang of jealousy. Those two were getting on a little too well. "We spoke to some of the crew there. They're all really excited about the reveal tomorrow."

"They're getting paid to say that," Dillon snarked, as she looked at the picture he'd taken of the Enclave. Even with Kyle's crappy photography, it looked foreboding.

"It's in there?"

Kyle's eyes went wide as he nodded. "And security is tight. They're seriously scared of whatever's in there. I don't think that's an act." He scrolled through the pictures of the security cameras he had taken around the park. "We counted a hundred and twelve new cameras encircling the Enclave. None of those were on the original plans we had." He handed the phone back to a middle-aged guy, Marv. He was a delivery driver and a geocaching enthusiast. He'd taken it upon himself to create a detailed schematic of the park.

He brushed the chips Dillon had tossed over his plans and, using the pictures' imbedded GPS coordinates to mark their exact position on the plans, he finished up placing tiny Xs on the map. Dillon could see from the clusters that he'd been busy.

"That's all of them, Marv declared."

Kyle studied it. "It's going to be tight, even if we all get in."

"We'll all get in," Dillon said confidently. She turned to Mike, a permanently angry Welshman who had the physique of a professional rugby player. "How're we doing on that?"

Mike crammed the rest of a burger into his mouth and pulled up a large set of plastic decals depicting a local plumbing company. "I ordered these from San Diego. They'll look smart when painted on." He nodded to a van. "We've been jamming the bog every day and they've finally called us in for tomorrow."

Kyle pulled a face. In his view, it was the weakest part of the entire operation, but Derek had insisted it would work, figuring that it always did in the movies. As an ex-cop, he had assured them that the mundane always went unchecked. While most of the team would arrive as paying guests, something that had only been achieved by spending an astronomical sum on black market tickets, they still needed to get the hardware in. Without that, there was no plan.

He ran his eyes over the map, processing all the many variables. "And are we confident about the power systems?"

Anna waved her hand dismissively. Her wrist was bound with an assortment of leather and cloth bracelets that immediately denounced her as an eco-warrior. "I downloaded the plans for the onsite power grid from City Hall." She leaned over the map, enjoying Kyle's lecherous look as she deliberately stretched to trace a power line coming into the western section of the park. "They have the main substation here, and three backup facilities here, here and here. The main station covers almost all the park. Shops, lights, everything. She pointed to one near the command hub. This is a key backup responsible for all the security systems. Including the cages and the SkyShield. But it's going to be difficult to get anywhere close."

"So, how do we take that one out?"

"We don't have to. It turns out if we take out the main station, these other two kick in. They're redundancies that split the load. So we take them down a minute after the first. That gives the system time to recalibrate and put the pressure on them and," she tapped the station near the command hub, "this becomes Big Daddy taking the strain. Then, BAM!" She slapped the table hard, causing everybody to jump. "We take the backups out at the same time. The sudden overload will then topple the entire system. It will burn itself out."

Dillon frowned. "Are you sure?"

"I ran the calcs myself. The system is designed for

gradual failures, not everything in one go. What's critical is our timing. They have to go in this sequence. Not only that, but we also have to do it when energy consumption is peak."

"Which is when?"

"Just as the park closes."

Kyle nodded his approval. "Good. We don't want the public getting hurt. Just those corporate assholes."

"Exactly. The kids'll be out. The cleaners will move in, drawing more power and, this is the kicker, all the lights come on until dawn. The place is lit up like a Christmas tree!" She bounced on the spot, delighted with herself.

Dillon was impressed, but determined not to show it. There was something about Anna's flippancy that irritated her. Despite her apparent air-headedness, Anna had studied civil engineering in college, which is what turned her towards the ideal of sustainable energy.

"And we have the muscle to do all of this?"

A wildly bearded guy sitting at the far end, drinking a Budweiser with his feet up on the table, gave a single nod. Zane was the only name he'd given. He was exactly the type of redneck Dillon's liberal senses instinctively loathed, yet he possessed a heart of gold. And accesses to an excessive array of firepower.

He planted a boot on several bricks of gray clay-like blocks, wrapped in paper. "Plastic explosives." A few of the team flinched, but Dillon knew it was inert until primed with a detonator. "Enough to blow a hole into their dimension," Zane purred, flashing a grin with far too many teeth missing. He held up a small metal cylinder. "These are the timers. I'll preset them all, so we've got to do is plant these." He patted the explosives, again causing people to jump. "Then get out." He lifted a brick and studied it closely. "I'm gonna carve these up so we can plant a few tiny charges around the enclosures."

"It won't harm the creatures, will it?" Dillon had expressed no concern about the plight of the guests, but she drew the line at harming the very animals they were trying to liberate.

Zane snickered. "I hear they can eat this stuff like Wile E. Coyote, explode, then reform. I ain't worried about them. But if they have trouble phasing in and out, I just wanna make sure a door lock isn't trapping them inside."

Dillon nodded in agreement. "Good idea. Particularly around the Enclave. I don't want to see any animal left behind."

The housewife, whose name eluded her, raised her hand. "What if they get shot trying to escape?"

Dillon smiled. "That's the beauty of bringing down the shields. Once they're down, they're free. Not just in this dimension. They can apport back home any time. They're not dumb. They won't wait around to be captured again."

Kyle clapped his hands and rubbed them together. "Great. This is all coming together. That just leaves the access passes to get in the secure areas."

Rishi, one of the India store clerks, spoke up. "I cloned the pass we stole." The police officer amongst them smiled and winked. He'd turned out to be a rather handy pick-pocket. Dillon didn't want to ask how he'd developed that skill.

She picked up a beer, but didn't pop the cap. She never drank. "Well done, guys! You've all done an outstanding job. It's time for us to do the right thing. Free those poor animals and make the corporate bastards who put them there pay."

The rest of the team broke into self-congratulatory applause. The big night was almost upon them.

Chapter 6

Tobias Elwood slouched in his chair as if it had been molded specifically for him. His easy lopsided grin was aimed squarely at the studio camera, guided by his instinct to always direct his good side towards a lens.

Sam Ebbs' tangle of red hair wobbled as the exuberant chat show host leaned forward across his desk.

"*Well, it terrifies me!*" he retorted to the loud laughter of his assembled audience.

Sitting on his couch at home, Wes stabbed the congealed mass of spaghetti and meatballs that he had over-nuked in the microwave.

"You hack…" he muttered under his breath.

"*… But that's the attraction of our new exhibit. It's the ultimate phantom.*"

"*Yet you somehow managed to capture it,*" Ebbs said to huge applause from the audience.

Elwood was embarrassed by the praise, but Wes recognized a bad actor when he saw one.

"*Well, somebody had to,*" Elwood said modestly.

Wes howled at the screen. "You mean an army of researchers, scientists, and your entire team? You ass-hat!"

"I don't know how you did it!" Ebbs cooed. *"And I believe this one is not like any of the others that have been discovered?"*

"That's right. The Satori Institute is just scraping the surface of what's out there, or over there!" He rode out the audience's sycophantic laughter. *"We had five classes of phantom,"* Elwood continued, *"and from II and up, they're all dangerous. The others are puppies. Harmless. Fun for the kids. But the other three get worse. And as we get to five, if you've seen my show, they're worse than specters and apparitions. I mean, they're smart and aggressive. But with our new boy, we had to create a sixth class. Think of it as phantom royalty."*

A loud hollow tock sound from the yard caught Wes's attention.

"It's the deadliest yet. And I know deadly. When I was a Marine—"

Wes muted the television. "You were still an asshole then," Wes muttered as the sound continued outside. He traded the bowl for his phone and cautiously edged towards the patio window. Although Spring Valley was a safe neighborhood in the west, this was still Vegas, home to the crazy, the egotistical, and the disenchanted.

His own yard was in darkness, but light pooled from Lisa's lounge, illuminating her standing at the edge of the beam with a baseball bat. Wes slid the door open, using his phone's flashlight to make sure he didn't step on anything that might bite or sting him – after all, beyond the back fence was nothing but desert. He stopped at the knee-high fence as Lisa picked up another rock and slogged it with the bat.

"Good swing," said Wes.

Lisa flinched in surprise and looked a little embarrassed at being caught.

"I hope I didn't wake you?"

He glanced at his Casio. It was five thirty. "I just got back home. Late shifts all-round. Big day tomorrow, um, tonight." It meant he wouldn't have his scheduled morning run-in with her, but this encounter was a bonus.

"Sure. I heard the commercial. Saw the ad. Repeatedly. And I had Sean hound me for the t-shirt and the new action figure." She picked up another rock and whacked it into the night.

"You missed your calling." She frowned. Wes pointed to the bat with his phone, almost blinding her with the flashlight. "Sorry." He turned the light off.

"Oh. I used to play with my dad and brother. They hated that I was better than them. Especially my dad. He was old school. Figured I should get married and kid-up. And I listened to him."

Whack! Another stone was launched into the ether.

Wes nodded sagely. "Judging by this excellent batswomanship, I would say your day was possibly worse than mine."

"Well, that's an interesting hypothesis. What was the worst thing that happened to you today?"

Getting burned by over-zealous ectoplasm excretions? The tedious monotony of sitting in the Banshee control booth watching tram after tram pass through, without the satisfaction of being able to study the fascinating creatures themselves? Being passed over for promotion yet again...

"We were just busy preparing for tonight. All hands to the deck."

"Sounds like a luxury compared to mine," Lisa pounded another rock. "I'm going to get fired because I chose the wrong gift bag."

Wes pretended to um-and-ah, then agreed she had had

the worst day. Lisa broke into a relieved laugh and tossed the bat down. She joined him at the fence.

"That sounds so lame out loud."

"It really does." That got a wider smile from her. Even with the weight of the world on her shoulders, and lack of sleep, he found her irresistible. "Care to elaborate, just so I can judge how lame your story it is?"

"Big clients flying in from China. Massive deal. We're trying to impress the hell out of them… and my wonderful boss thinks I have screwed the deal already. I spent all day on the phone trying to source something just right to impress them."

"And what did you pick?"

"It's still a toss-up between a voucher for Arby's or a ride on the coaster at New York-New York."

"Classy."

The fabulous, tortured smile faded, and her gaze drifted to the floor. "So first thing tomorrow…" she looked at her watch. "Or rather, in five hours' time. I either look for a job in the Casinos… or I finally get the hell out of here."

"You don't like Vegas?"

"It's not the sort of place you want to bring up children." With a sigh. She looked introverted. "Do you ever think that you chose the wrong path in life? Just that one fork in fate's road that only now you can see so clearly would've made everything so much better?"

"All the time." Wes immediately regretted the enthusiastic reply. She didn't notice.

Lisa forced a weary smile. "Any jobs going at your place?"

Wes laughed. Then was struck by a thought.

"Why don't you bring your clients to the launch tonight?"

The idea clearly hadn't occurred to her. "I thought it was sold out?"

"Sure, to the average joe, but there are always VIP tickets."

Her face lit up with hope. "And you can get them? For a party of five?"

Wes knew he was making pale promises, but the look she wore was beyond adorable.

"Of course." He forced a grin. "I keep telling you, I'm an essential player there."

A flicker of doubt crossed her face as she glanced at his house. It wasn't the cheapest accommodation in town, but not far from it.

"Oh, this?" Wes waved a dismissive hand. "It was an Airbnb thing when I moved… then I've just been too busy to relocate…" He held up his phone and cycled through to the selfie Elwood took. "I mean, this says it all."

Her doubt faded. "Cool. Boy, you look pissed off."

"Oh, he has that effect on me."

Lisa's brain was now working overtime. "When does the park open?"

"Tonight it's a little different because it's Halloween. We're opening at sunset."

Lisa nodded thoughtfully. "That gives us the whole day for discussions… and I can paint this as a trip to celebrate the deal. That makes us sound confident."

"Sure does," said Wes, regretting his rash decision with every passing second. If he couldn't pull his promise off, then he'd just got her fired.

"Oh. What about the kids?"

Wes's desire to impress derailed the escape clause he'd just been handed. "No problem. I have two complimentary tickets. They can hang with me."

He felt his stomach knot.

Lisa threw her arms around him and hugged him tight. His face was buried in her soft blonde hair, and a musky smell filled his nostrils, arousing him. It was something that he didn't want to end.

Lisa let go. "Wes, if you can do this, you'd be my hero for life!"

He felt dizzy and almost unable to breathe. He started to pull himself together to tell her the truth.

Instead, he found himself nodded and saying: "Sure. It's not a problem!"

After a fitful sleep, Wes left early for his Halloween shift, clocking in at three, a full four hours before opening night. He'd barely slept as he tried to work out a way to undo his tangle of lies, but he couldn't face the shame in admitting the truth to Lisa.

Already the park was buzzing with crews preparing for the Enclave's opening. Halloween decorations were in every window, hung from every lamppost. For the last twenty-three hours, teams had been combing through the park, ensuring everything looked perfect.

Wes knew he only had one chance to score the tickets he needed. He'd have to swallow his pride and turn to the only man who could apparently do the impossible. He picked his ambush position at the Imp Aviary and pretended to test the cage's security.

Beyond the throbbing translucent screen was a junkyard diorama, with a couple of smashed cars and a jet engine still attached to a wing, surrounded by various aircraft detritus. The engine originally had a motor turning the blades, but the imps had soon gnawed that apart.

They were a subspecies of gremlins. Leathery-winged and reptilian, they perched inquisitively on their rear legs, tails constantly swishing. Their bodies were adorned with a patchwork of chameleon-like scales that allowed them to blend into their environments when resting. They had a taste for metal, particularly copper wiring, which often led to horrific accidents.

Wes liked them. Behaviorally, they were one of the more interesting pan-species and quite innocuous, save for the mildly paralyzing saliva that occasionally caused an anaphylactic shock.

"Ready for the big day?"

Wes watched as a six-foot purple cartoon ghost walking towards him. It was the park's mascot, Phamo. He removed his head – a forbidden act when guests were in – to reveal the pimply teenager beneath.

"Hey, Stuart. As ready as I'll ever be."

Stuart mistook Wes's distracted tone for work related stress. "I'm sure it'll all go like clockwork." He weighed Phamo's head in his hands. "They got us rehearsing a new dance routine. It's crazy. I keep forgetting the steps."

"You poor bastard." Wes wondered if he had finally met somebody lower on the chain than he was. They'd been friends since Wes joined. Like him, Stuart had ambitions to join the hunting team. A jealous part of him suspected he'd achieve it, too.

"This place is sure looking good, though." Stuart pointed across the Mexican plaza, replicating where the imps had been found, except this one was brightly painted in red, yellow and orange, and every single building was an overpriced gift store or food outlet. Window displays were being remodeled with Halloween themed merchandise, and sweatshirts with Elwood firing a vapo and the words: *Time to Fry!*

Stuart was clearly impressed. "Seen his new action

figure?" Wes nodded glumly. "The Vaporizer even lights up! You know you've made it when you've got a four-inch posable plastic figure of yourself. It's the ultimate status symbol."

"Do you ever think this is all wrong?"

"What d'you mean?"

"CERN finally provides evidence of parallel worlds. An epoch-making discovery. It's on every news channel around the planet, and the first thing we do with this revolutionary knowledge is open a freakin' theme park so we can all gawp at them." Stuart laughed, clearly loving the idea. Wes shook his head sadly. "Whatever happened to gaining knowledge for the sake of it?"

"You're starting to sound like one of those animal rights weirdos. What's wrong with making some money on the side?"

Wes was riled up to argue. He was feeling bitter enough, and Stuart was an easy target. Fortunately, he was distracted when Elwood marched across the plaza talking on his phone. Right on schedule. Stuart was still talking when Wes jogged to catch up with Elwood.

"Elwood! Your big day."

Elwood hung up and vaguely waved his phone. "Worthless agent's trying to negotiate with stupid networks. She's supposed to be tough, so why isn't she getting me what I want?" He was treating it like a personal affront. "I tell you, if you ever get your own show, give it some serious thought. It's so much hassle."

"I imagine it makes life really difficult for you."

Realizing Wes was keeping pace, he looked sidelong at him. "West, isn't it?"

"Wes. Yesterday we spoke about my application to the hunting team."

"Right." His vagueness was loud and clear; he'd already forgotten.

"Sure. And you said you'd make it up to me with the corporate tickets I needed for tonight."

"Tickets…?"

Wes zeroed in on his confusion. "Thank God you didn't forget. It was those folks from the network I mentioned."

"Which network?"

Wes smoothly glossed over the details. "They needed to see you in person. You were quite excited by it."

Elwood frowned in confusion. Wes steamrolled over the silence.

"Who was it you said I needed to talk to in guest services?" Wes circled a finger, pretending to recall the name. "They were really keen you did this…"

"Grace sorts all my stuff out," Elwood said, his confusion evaporating as another call came in. "My agent."

Wes stopped in his tracks, thankful not to spend any more time with the walking ego. "Of course. Grace. She might call you to confirm this is legit." Elwood waved him away. "Cool. See you tonight."

Elwood was already arguing with his agent. Wes spun on his heels and hurried towards guest services in the admin building. Armed with the selfie on his phone, he was sure he could get this all sewn up in the next half hour. He just hoped that Calvin wouldn't notice he'd been missing from his scheduled duties.

Chapter 7

"Just remember how important this is for me," Lisa hissed between her teeth as she crushed her children's hands until they whimpered. They were already tugging like eager bloodhounds as they eyed the park's entrance gate.

"Don't embarrass me," Sean said indignantly. He had been a volcano of joy since Lisa had told them Wes's news, although as usual they'd already argued as she'd forced him to leave behind a backpack of merchandise that he wanted Elwood to sign. He'd been limited to his latest illustrated phantom encyclopedia. Emma had been far more reserved when greeting the news, but she had lapsed into wide-eyed, breathless excitement and had hardly uttered a word all day.

Lisa glanced at her watch. It was just after six thirty; the sun had officially set, but it wasn't quite dark, and crowds were already swarming into the park and there was still no sign of Wes. His only confirmation to her barrage of text messages had been a thumbs-up and the time. She prayed she hadn't misinterpreted him. Clarkson was delighted with her last-minute scoop, and she had been granted a reprieve from his bile. As the day wore on, the negotiations had passed with ease. Clarkson mellowed, and she had become increasingly anxious. She'd feel easier if she had the tickets in her hand. Her stress increased when she saw the stretch limo carrying Clarkson and the four Chinese delegates rolling towards the VIP drop-off area. She hoped a good day would not be brought crashing down...

"There he is!" Emma squealed as she pointed at Wes. He wore heavily soiled coveralls as he dashed from a staff entrance.

Relief flooded through Lisa, and she felt like kissing him. He was a short, wiry and *very far* from her usual type. Yet the shock of curly brown hair and twinkling dark eyes made him seem youthful. There was an awkward charm there, something that made her smile.

He spun around twice before spotting her. He ran across, brandishing a black envelope.

"There you go!"

Lisa motioned to embrace him, but stopped short when she smelled the acrid stench of ectoplasm. She noticed the flash of disappointment on his face as she recoiled.

"Is that ghost puke?" Emma asked as the plasm fizzed on his uniform.

"It's ectoplasm!" Sean's finger was on its way to poking a blob. Wes caught his hand.

"I wouldn't touch it. It burns like fu... like heck."

Lisa released her children and took possession of the envelope. "Guys, from now on you listen to Wes. He's in charge. Understand?"

"It's okay, mom, ectoplasm is a bio-plasma compound made by the sudden excitement of–"

"Wes is the expert! Listen to him." Her attention was already on the limo as it pulled to the sidewalk.

"You know your stuff," Wes beamed at Sean.

"I learned from the best."

Wes grinned. "Oh, thanks…" but trailed away when Sean held up Elwood's book.

"Can you ask him to sign it?"

Lisa zoned out of the conversation as Clarkson stepped from the limo, quickly followed by Mofa Quantum's president, Charles Lei, with his CFO and their translator. The Chinese entrepreneur's face was stretched in a delighted smile as he took in the impressive entrance. At thirty-five, he had already started a unicorn company specializing in easy cell phone payments that could be used by anybody from the rich to farmers in third-world countries. He had sold that off to start Mofa Quantum. Born in Shanghai, education in Oxford, he was far from the prim and stuffy Asian businessman Lisa had been expecting. Even during disagreements, he smiled. Whether it was a trick to disarm his opponent or genuine enjoyment from negotiating, she couldn't tell. He laughed constantly and humbly acknowledged every person in the room. Even the interns. He was a new generation of entrepreneur with a fresh new attitude she approved of. The polar opposite of her boss.

She nudged Wes's elbow to indicate he should follow, then hurried across to greet them.

"Mister Lei, welcome to Phantom Land. I would like to introduce you to one of the key staff here. Wes Talasky."

She saw Wes freeze as Charles extended his hand. "Mr Talasky, a pleasure. And what is your function here?"

Alarmed, Wes glanced at Lisa and caught Sean and Emma watching him closely. Lisa suddenly felt guilty that she didn't know exactly what Wes did, either. He was always coy, and the park had a formidable culture of secrecy. Perhaps she should have pre-warned him?

Wes found his voice as he shook hands. "I'm a facilitations manager."

"And what does that entail?"

"It's about practical application of technology in the exhibits…" he said vaguely.

Charles took a step closer and lowered his voice conspiratorially. "I understand. Miss Mammott delighted me when she mentioned you could facilitate my visit on this day of all days."

Clarkson squirmed his way between the men. "Actually, that was my idea, Charlie. I wanted to offer you a unique experience. Something you can tell your grandkids about. You were here when they unveiled phantom royalty."

Charles guffawed. "And I feared my visit would be plagued by tiresome gift bags! A sign of a weak imagination." He took Wes's elbow and angled him a few paces to the side. "Miss Mammott also told me you are close friends with Tobias Elwood."

"I can't get rid of him."

"I would very much like to meet him. Perhaps a personal few moments to get his impression on the new exhibit?"

Lisa tensed. She hadn't been expecting yet another favor. Wes shot her a look, and she resisted the urge to bleat an apology. Luckily, Wes shrugged and flashed a half-smile she found adorable.

"We'll be busy… but let's see what I can work out."

Clarkson indicated to the entrance. "Charles, why don't we look around? You know, I haven't been here myself."

The group turned their collective backs on Wes and walked towards the gates. Lisa followed with a last glance over her shoulder. She silently mouthed '*thank you.*'

Wes watched them enter the park before remembering

that Sean and Emma were still at his side, looking at him with pent-up excitement.

"Mommy's boss is a jerk," confided Emma. "He calls up all the time. At night, too. He's always shouting."

"Well, let's hope this helps her out."

Sean tugged Wes's sleeve. "Are we going to go in now or what?"

Blake paced the command hub, scanning the array of images on the master screen and daring something to go awry. Since opening day, they'd added eight new major exhibits, each placing increasing pressure on the system. However, baring minor glitches, everything had run like clockwork. He anticipated that tonight's launch would be harder work than all combined. It was both a testament to his management skills and his team that it was going so smoothly. And that was making for an incredibly dull evening.

It was now dark outside, and the park was coming to life as more guests flooded in.

"Ninety-eight percent capacity," Hugh Pine said as the occupancy figures ticked upwards. Linked to the cameras across the park, the AI systems counted every man, woman and child with such accuracy that when compared to the ticket tally, even people who sneaked in could be accounted for.

"Make sure we close the gates on one-hundred."

Hugh nodded. "Will do. Publicity is monitoring numbers too."

"Why?"

"So they can notify the press the moment people are turned away." Tanaka saw the puzzled look on his boss's face. "We've *never* been at maximum capacity. They say it's perfect PR for the new exhibit."

"Jesus Christ." Blake shook his head. Image was everything.

"They're so neat!" Emma exclaimed, watching the imps flutter across the aviary in graceful arcs before alighting on the gouged remains of a truck. They gnawed into the metal with their tiny incisors.

Sean nodded impatiently, torn between fascination and the burning desire to see more. He glanced at Wes, who was scrolling through the park app on his phone.

"Wes, can we see the specters now?"

"Um, I guess. But these little guys are really fascinating. People always overlook them. But—"

"They're okay, but we wanna see the *big* stuff."

Wes didn't know quite what he expected from the kids, but his app had been buzzing constantly for the last twelve minutes. Calvin was monitoring him, and with duties missed and the GPS tracking pinpointing his exact location, Wes was running out of excuses. He silenced the app.

The plaza was packed with families riding on adrenaline

from their last encounter, or struggling to restrain their sugar-fueled kids charging into gift shops. He spotted Phamo posing for pictures with grinning teenagers.

"Hey, how about a picture with Phamo?"

Sean rolled his eyes, leaving him in no doubt that was at the bottom of his wish list.

"Maybe we should find mom?" Emma said, finally tiring of the imps.

The thought of a bad report to Lisa sent a shock wave through Wes. It would undo the whole point of this badly thought-out pretense. His phone buzzed again.

The sight of a tour tram gave him hope. It was a shorter train of two cars and unlike the other white bodied vehicles, this one was polished black with stylized gold trim. The upholstered seats offered comfort, unlike the regular ass-numbing fiberglass numbers. It had VIP written into its engineering.

Tobias Elwood sat in a jump seat in the front carriage, facing the adoring crowd as he gave a coveted personal tour. Dressed in a casual black windcheater, embossed with the Park's logo, it failed to cover the t-shirt of himself underneath. It also struggled to contain the muscles that swelled in each arm as he animatedly talked. His mere presence was charming his captive audience of Clarkson, Charles Lei, and the rest of the Mofa Quantum posse. Lisa was right at the back, eyes wide with wonder as they pulled up at the aviary. Elwood recited his Mexican adventures.

What gave Wes hope was the driver. It was a rather bored Kirk. Robbed of his usual rapport with the guests, he stared glumly at the bag of Cheetos on his lap. Wes snatched Sean's and Emma's hands, pulling them forward.

"Come on!"

"That's Tobias Elwood!" breathed Emma, pointing ahead in hero worship.

"That's right," said Wes. "I told you that you'd get to meet him."

He intercepted the tram as Kirk triggered the onboard narration and picked at the Cheetos, several packets of which would power him through the night. He was sucking his stained orange fingers when Wes caught up.

"Kirk, remember that favor you owe me?"

"Uh, no…"

"Well, I'm cashing in." Wes hoisted Emma into the jump seat next to Kirk.

"Guests can't come up here. Wes! This is a freakin' VIP tour."

"These are VIP guests. Remember the lady I may have mentioned in the past…" his words dripped with meaning as he shunted Sean to the other side of the cab. "The one I got tickets for tonight?"

Realization dawned on Kirk's face as Wes indicated to the back of the tram. As discreetly as a chainsaw, Kirk craned around in his seat and saw Lisa in profile. "Oh, the neighbor you want to ban… bring," he quickly corrected himself as Emma smiled at him. "Nice. And you're playing the kid card?"

"What does that mean?" asked Emma suspiciously.

"Nothing," snapped Wes, shooting Kirk a look that warned him to shut up. "They're really looking forward to this." Wes jiggled his phone meaningfully as it vibrated again. "I have an urgent call out…"

Kirk's index finger gave a half-hearted salute. "Gotcha. Two kids, two favors."

"Anything."

Kirk held up his hand for both children to high-five.

"I'm Kirk, and it looks like I'm gonna be your personal guide through Phantom Land."

"We get to ride up here?" asked Sean, his eyes wide.

"Sure thing!"

Sean craned around to see Elwood was within arm's reach. He was finishing an anecdote that had everybody laughing.

"And Tobias Elwood is showing us around?"

Kirk swapped a look with Wes. Star power had a way of sucking the fun out of everything. "Sure. If you like."

Wes flashed them a thumbs-up. "Darn right! I've got some urgent hunter business to attend to."

"That's right," said Kirk with a grin and a look that suggested the list of favors he expected from Wes was now on an ever-increasing meter. "Wes is a real hotshot around here. So you get to stay with me. *For a little while.*" The last was delivered heavily, for Wes's benefit.

"Just make sure they see everything."

Kirk ran out of time to argue as Elwood's narration drew to a close and he thumbed the button indicating the tram should move on. The indicator on Kirk's screen blinked, and the park's schematic told him that another tram was already waiting to take his spot. He tapped the pedal to move on.

Nobody paid Wes any attention as the tram pulled away, even Elwood, who was looking right through him. At the last moment, Lisa noticed him and did a double take. She smiled and waved. Wes gave her a thumbs-up and immediately regretted the dumb response. He indicated to the front of the tram. Lisa saw her children and a warm smile cracked her face. She looked back towards Wes, but he'd disappeared from view as the tram mounted the slipway, cutting deeper into the park.

Chapter 8

Kyle's fingers nervously drummed on the steering wheel. Dillon waited until the guard turned away to check his screen in the gate booth, before she reached across and crushed his fingers so tightly that he whimpered in pain. They both wore grubby t-shirts, jeans, and green high-visibility jackets.

"Act casual," she hissed.

He snorted and yanked his hand free to take the ID from the guard.

"Thanks." Kyle flashed a smile, which the guard didn't return. He handed him a printed map with a highlighted route.

"This will take you to maintenance parking. Then take one of the buggies to the C23 toilet block. Make sure you read all the health and safety instructions on the back."

Kyle nodded amiably and slowly drove the van through the gate when the barrier lifted. He heard a pent-up breath escape Dillon's lips. Once they turned onto the maintenance ring road that orbited the park, she turned in her seat, kneeling to address the four other team members huddled under a blanket in the back.

"We're in!"

Derek, the ex-cop, repositioned his glasses as he sat up. The idea to disguise themselves as plumbers had been his idea. It had been vetoed several times as being too dumb a ploy to gain admittance. It had taken a presentation – a full PowerPoint presentation – on human psychology to convince them. As a cop, he'd learned that most people ignored a fluorescent yellow jacket, beloved by marshals and construction workers around the globe. It attracted attention and demanded to be seen, so people naturally assumed jacketed people were supposed to be there.

"Told you it would. An oldie, but a goodie."

Kamala, who had introduced herself as a homemaker to a good doctor husband, turned out to run a moderately successful online store supplying hard to find ingredients for Oriental food, ruffled her jet-black hair and shot Derek a dubious look.

"If it hadn't, and they shot me, I swear I would've come back to haunt you!"

That provoked a snort of laughter from Moran, a forty-something store clerk who had been one of the first to join the cause. He looked around at everybody else's questioning looks.

"What? It's funny. We now know ghosts aren't dead people," he held out his arms zombie fashion and slurred his words. "So that's amusing."

"Don't get me started on that!" intoned Mike in a thick Welsh accent. "I bloody ran a successful stately guesthouse in Merthyr Tydfil, didn't I? Most bloody haunted place in the UK. Then," he snapped his fingers, "out of business overnight when they discover these bastards are like rats sneaking into our dimension. Environmental Health closed me down! And they have the nerve to open up this bloody theme park when me family business went bust, just like that!" He snapped his fingers again.

Unlike the others, Mike didn't care about the imprisoned creatures, he just wanted to see the park put out of business. His loss had deeper personal ramifications with the bankruptcy and a divorce that quickly followed. It was a weighty vendetta he carried on his shoulders.

"Well, despite my reservations, your plan worked, Derek. Congratulations." Dillon put on a baseball cap, complete with a stylized plumbing logo Mike had created: *Gungebusters*. "Jenna and Marv just messaged," she habitually glanced at her phone. "Everybody is in. You all know the drill. One orbit round handing out the explosives. Then get them positioned as fast as possible. But don't take any risks. If a place looks too hot, move on and come back to it later. This is not a sightseeing excursion. Zane double checked every timer, so don't alter a thing." She held a detonator up and indicted to a small switch on top. "Arm it with this, then leave. We should all be safely back in bed by the time this hits the morning news."

Everybody nodded and began double-checking their equipment. Kyle had made them check before they left. Despite his hippy facade, he had the desiccated heart of a military drill instructor.

Dillon passionately pounded her fist against the seat's headrest. "Remember, these phantoms are real creatures. They deserve our respect. It doesn't matter where they come from, they have rights to be free and not held prisoner for our entertainment." She was happy with the serious nods in reply, all except Mike, who just grimaced. "Animals have rights. We do this for them!"

She raised her fist, anticipating a jubilant cheer. All she got in reply were solemn nods. The van gently rocked as Kyle pulled up in their designated parking space. Dillon raised her phone again. "We're all on WhatsApp. Any problems notify the team. So, let's go and unleash some freedom!"

The yawning cave mouth looked like a grotesque mouth in the bleak Irish landscape. A perfectly designed crooked tree beckoned the way onward into the Banshee Tunnels.

Kirk slowly drove towards the dark tunnel. Whistling wind and the cry of starving ravens played out through a fully immersive atmospheric sound mix, adding to the tension. He stifled a yawn. The banshees were one of his favorites, and always good for getting impressionable young girls swooning in his arms. But tonight he was redundant, as Tobias Elwood would run the show. Plus, he had had little sleep as he'd left the park the previous night with one of the guests, a twenty-year-old SoCal girl who had taken a shine to him after freaking out in the Bogeyman experience. A strong arm, a soft smile, and some cheesy lines usually got them into bed afterwards. And now he was suffering from partying from 4am until lunchtime.

"Plug your bladders, people!" snapped Elwood across the PA system in what he considered were tense tones. "Next up is really scary. We're entering the caves of Ireland and sinking into the dreaded Banshee Tunnels!"

Sean and Emma exchanged wide-eyed looks; their mouths open.

"This is so cool!" Sean hissed. Then tapped Kirk's arm to get his attention. "Do they scare you?"

"Nah, not anymore." Kirk flashed a cocky smile, although that wasn't quite true. The pan's ability to provoke fear wasn't something that diminished much. He'd recently seen a video of a wild banshee's sonic scream on YouTube before it had been taken down. Watching the skin flayed from somebody's face was an image he couldn't unseen.

Sean twisted in his seat and saw Elwood's back was just within reach. He tapped him on the shoulder. Elwood gave a double take as he turned, expecting to see Kirk alone.

"Mr Elwood," Sean hissed. "You're awesome!"

The flattery overrode any safety concerns Elwood had. "Thanks kid."

Sean held up his book and a Sharpie. "Can you sign this?"

A flicker of annoyance flashed across Elwood's face. "Sure." He snatched the pen and automatically signed his flamboyant signature. He passed it back and made a circling motion with his finger. "Eyes front. We're going in!"

Everything went black as they entered the tunnel. Kirk's screen dimmed, and he released the wheel, taking his foot off the pedal as they came to a stop. But there was still a sense of movement. Sean's eyes adjusted to see the walls were moving past them and realized they had parked on a moving conveyor that carried the tram forward.

Lightning suddenly tore overhead, and a huge cyclorama faded into existence, with swirling animated storm clouds. As far as the eye could see, lay fields of dry wheat blowing in the breeze. The line between physical props and the enormous LED screens was impossible to define. More lightning revealed a crooked scarecrow and a dilapidated farmhouse as the centerpiece.

"Folklore says banshees hounded the dying," intoned Elwood over the PA.

Another flash of lightning revealed four gaunt figures circling the farmhouse and zigzagging between the trees. Sean gasped and pointed. Emma had already seen them, her eyes wide with fascination and fear.

"To hear their screams would herald your death. But these were no old wives' tales or legends. They are real. A banshee's scream is death itself. A sonic scream that can tear flesh from bone."

Opposite the farmhouse, the tram stopped moving.

More lightning flickered and the banshees suddenly switched direction and headed for the tram at speed. Sean and Emma just had time to make out withered humanoid features; gaunt faces and hollow eyes giving them a hag-like appearance. Their thin bodies tapered into nothing, with emancipated arms ending in curved five-inch talons. Matted fur gave the fleeting impression they were clad in ancient robes.

It took seconds before the beasts were suddenly upon the tram. Everybody screamed as a banshee wail rose around them.

It was a sensation similar to having water lodged in the ears. It caused a wave of dizziness, chilled the blood, and raised goosebumps over their bodies. Each sensation unpleasantly overlapped the other in the space of seconds.

The banshees were feet away – ready for the kill.

Then the creatures hit an invisible wall which flashed purple with each impact. Sean could now see the Tesla shield ran through the hoops arching overhead, following the tram's path. It was like standing in an aquarium tunnel with death just inches away.

The first wave of screams was replaced by embarrassed laughter from the guests. Sean felt himself go giddy as his ears unblocked. A glut of hormones had been released from them all as adrenaline surged their systems. That was the beauty of Phantom Land. It could replicate physical and emotional experiences no roller coaster could, and certainly nothing virtual reality could hold a torch to. This was hard-wired fight-or-flight mechanics and, as many guests had discovered. It was an addictive natural high.

Elwood chuckled as everybody relaxed, although they still flinched. Then the banshees repeatedly struck the tunnel wall, desperate to reach their prey.

"Don't worry, folks. That was just a recording of a banshee wail. Luckily for us, the harmonics in the real scream don't record too well, so you're perfectly safe. And the tunnel is soundproof, so they can whine all they like. The interesting thing here is that they can't scream in flight, so you're only in jeopardy when they land. And, for reasons we're still figuring out, *hearing* those harmful frequencies triggers your head to basically implode."

Sean saw the banshees' mouths hyper-extending like snakes' jaws as they silently screamed at their targets. He glanced back to see everybody was watching in awe. Even his mother was impressed, even though she had never sat down to watch a full episode of Spook Hunters with them.

"Like all pans," Elwood continued, "they feed primarily on fear. Naturally, these guys also have a taste for something more organic. Not flesh and blood, which their scream strips away, but the calcium in your bones and the bone marrow within. It's a delicacy for a banshee."

With a clatter, a concealed chute deposited a mass of

cow bones in front of the tram. The banshees immediately zeroed in on them, landing on the floor and awkwardly crawling closer, vulture-like, on their slender limbs.

"You may have seen Spook Hunters, episode six, when I caught these bad boys near Cork in Ireland. Nasty business." His voice dropped, betraying a modicum of emotion. "We lost Kenny, the sound guy on that show…"

Sean glanced at Elwood and was surprised to see he looked sad. It was fleeting, but left Sean in no doubt that the rumors he had read online about that particular episode were true. His head exploded, all caught on camera.

Sean looked back at the banshees as a pair squabbled over a leg bone that shattered in a single powerful bite. He could easily believe such stories.

Purple ectoplasm sizzled on the shovel, releasing a sulfuric odor that turned Wes's stomach. He dropped the load into a wheelbarrow and set about scraping the rest of the mucus from the wall, aware of the gaggle of visitors watching.

The specters were behind a Tesla partition, keeping them cornered in the enclosure. They hovered, quietly hissing through needle teeth. Luminescent eyes watched with ruthless predator cunning. They were calm, forever assessing. They had been acting oddly all evening. Every time a guest got close, they would all strike the same spot on the screen in rapid succession, as if testing for a weakness.

Wes felt caught in the spotlight as he eyed the guests staring at him. Knowing that he was on Calvin's shit-list, and the park employed mystery guests to provoke trouble and improve the experience, you never knew who was watching. He forced a smile and addressed them.

"I'll soon be finished up, folks." He watched a small child stare at him with as much indifference as she could summon. "And don't worry, specters are quite at home in confined spaces. Our exhibits here have become smart pack hunters, as I'm sure you saw. Ordinarily, they'd hunt solo." He jerked the shovel in their direction. "These little ones are Scandinavian. If you go out to the paddock in the south, you'll see the bigger ones found in Africa. And then there're the Russians. They're the worst." He indicated to the traces of ectoplasm on the door panel. "They've been using ecto-plasm excretions to see if they can short the door controls." He felt some satisfaction when the adults flicked apprehen-sive looks at the critters.

Wes inflated his chest, deploying the Tobias Elwood smooth smile technique, which he couldn't quite pull off. "But don't worry folks, spookologists like me are the real experts here at the park. We know all their tricks."

He picked up a hosepipe and sent a stream of water at the specters. They flinched and scattered sideways with a low hiss. The water sizzled and evaporated on the Tesla screen.

"You're hurting it!" wailed the bored child, suddenly alert with concern.

"Impossible. Just annoying it. They hate water and won't cross it. The frequency of the screens here, at six-giga-hertz means—"

He saw the bored child's eyes widened, looking beyond him. He spun around to see one specter speeding towards the screen where it was still crackling with ectoplasm. It slammed into the energy sheet. Instead of being repelled, the beast's shoulder wedged through it. Less than half an inch, but the warty brown skin was clearly visible on the other side.

And that was supposed to be impossible.

Wes's shock was momentary. The exposed skin glistened as a fist-sized globule of ectoplasm excreted from it. Wes barely had time to raise his arms. The hose took the brunt of the projectile and the gloop sizzled on his forearms. Luckily, the uniform's special coating would protect his skin, and his eyes were shielded by protective goggles. But that was new, undocumented behavior.

"What the hell…" he muttered.

The shield regained its integrity, and the specter was bounced back into the pack. The audience burst into laughter. Still reeling in shock, and wondering how the water could have possibly weakened the shield, Wes forced a smile.

"See what I mean? They're always looking for an opportunity to tear you apart."

He carefully finished putting the cleaning materials away, taking extra care to wipe the slime from his arm. He was relieved to step from the enclosure and released the specters from confinement. Now the crowd was distracted, watching them prowl, and Wes was all but forgotten as he stood to the side, wiping residual crap from his arm.

"Ain't that your Talasky, fella?"

Wes looked up to see the VIP tram had slowed past the enclosure and Clarkson was pointing at him.

"That's nobody. Just one of my janitorial staff showing just why you shouldn't get into a cage with a ghost!" laughed Elwood, pointing an accusing finger. "Don't forget to shower, West, or you'll stink worse than usual all week."

The tram passed with rapturous laughter. Wes saw Sean leaning from the driver's cabin, looking confused. It was a look that was the death knell of any hero-worship the kids had.

As the tram rolled onwards towards the Enclave, Lisa slid into his field of view. Her expression one of bewilderment. Had his lies had just been exposed? It made him feel sick inside, and he suddenly wished the specter had got him square in the face instead...

Chapter 9

Sarah Dillon couldn't take her eyes from the spud-like creature bobbing through the enclosure like a balloon cause in a zephyr. The area was swarming with younger children who stretched to reach for them, but the carefully concealed energy screens kept the phantoms at arm's length. A young spookologist, who couldn't be more than twenty, her hair held back in long pigtails, beamed a thousand-watt smile as she told the kids the Class I phantoms were relatively dumb and harmless. Unless you were a bird or stray pet.

The kids, Dillon couldn't help but notice with disdain, wore nothing but designer gear paid for by parents who wouldn't normally spend so much time with them in a month, as they were this very evening.

"Poor thing," she mumbled as a phantom rebounded from the shield and helplessly spiraled, as if caught in a river current. "We'll get you out, buddy."

She suddenly felt a wave of dizziness. It was a nauseous sensation she'd been experiencing since entering the park. At first, she thought it was the tension that had been building during the weeks leading up to liberation. It felt similar to liberating caged bonobos from a research lab in San Francisco. That had nearly resulted in her being caught. Two of the protestors had been imprisoned, and the poor bonobos had been rounded up and euthanized after mauling a security guard.

Another raid at a zoo in New Orleans had yielded similar results, although some of the freed animals had vanished into the wild. It was unfortunate that a rare sable had been found in the contents of a snared alligator, but she felt that she'd won a moral victory.

However, this time the nausea was more pronounced. Perhaps it was a touch of fever. She swore she could hear the vaguest of whispers just on the edge of comprehension. She wouldn't be surprised if she'd caught something in the crowded casinos. Vegas was a cesspit she'd be happy to leave.

She met up with Kyle at the east perimeter wall and eyed a concealed gate, behind which lay one of the electrical substations. A few guests passed, ignoring their bright fluorescent jackets. Dillon felt invisible. She took the cloned access pass from her jacket and held it over the security lock. They'd soon know if Rishi's cloned pass would work. He was confident it would. He'd convinced them all he was a skilled hacker, a part of the Anonymous hacktivist group, but he provided no evidence. Dillon's doubts were further raised when he swore he'd been involved in helping expose a secret plan to lace the sky with mind-altering chemtrails. That had convinced her he was one of the internet's nut jobs.

The lock turned green, and the latched clicked open.

"It works," she said in surprise.

Kylie hurriedly shoved her through.

The substation lay a hundred yards down an access road. There were cameras here, but if anybody was watching them, then they weren't raising the alarm. Beyond the gray cinder block building, five massive metal transformer towers sucked in the current from suspended power lines. They hummed with electrical menace. A further mass of wires fed directly into the building, which was accessible by a set of steps leading down to another locked door. Again, Rishi's magic pass allowed them access.

The substation itself was warmer than the outside air. The advanced air-cooling system kept the huge main transformer, which dominated the room, at an even temperature.

Kyle wobbled and pinched the bridge of his nose.

"Are you okay?" she asked, steadying him.

It took him a moment before he nodded. His normally buoyant attitude had faded since entering the park.

"Sure. This place just gives me the creeps."

"It's supposed to. Remember why we're doing this. This whole place is designed to give those poor animals a bad rep."

He nodded, but didn't seem as convinced as he had done.

Dillon lightly shook his arm. "Keep it together. They're just animals caged by a hostile art department. They won't hurt anybody. They don't want to be here either. All of this is all propaganda against the little guy."

She had often fantasized about hanging up her liberation boots and opening a food company that somehow enabled people to feed from emotions. It was a talent the pan-dimensional spooks had, and one she suspected would be a new culinary revolution.

Their phones chimed with a message. Mike was in position outside the Enclave and ready to move in to plant his charges. Zane and Sarah had reached another substation. Dillon texted back a thumbs-up emoji.

"Come on, let's wire this place up and head over to the Wight Paddock. Then we can all go home."

Kyle nodded and followed her lead as she carefully took a lump of plastic explosive from her satchel and placed it at the base of the transformer.

So far, so good.

Michael Jones was permanently furious. From the moment his business had collapsed, and he'd lost the dream mansion that he'd bought with his wife, his temper had become uncontrollable. These days he lashed out at everybody around. Which is exactly why Eve, attempting to endure their failing business with calm dignity, had finally snapped and divorced him.

All because of a sodding ghost.

The poltergeist had been a playful attraction, often manifesting in the bar to tip a punter's pint over or shake the shelves. One time it had tried to pull the TV off the wall during a rugby match between Wales and France. That hadn't gone down well with the punters. But on the whole, it was a playful supernatural entity that attracted visitors.

Within three months of scientists discovering ghosts, ghouls and specters were not only real animals, but could drift between our world and a parallel one, his business had suffered.

Suddenly, people like Tobias Elwood were on television, plucking the beasts from the darkest corners and revealing them to the world for what they really were: ugly, weird, but somehow living animals. Naturally, the desire to suddenly sleep in a haunted house became as attractive as staying in a rat-infested hotel. The playful poltergeist went from a supernatural inconvenience to an infestation. And it was no longer as impressive as a Class V phantom scaring the bejesus out of people on TV.

Eight months after the major scientific discovery, Mike and Eve were filing for bankruptcy. By the time the foundation stone for Phantom Land was laid, their divorce proceedings had started. The first building hadn't even been erected before he lost everything.

His anger had drawn him to online anti-phantom protest groups. Spending far too much time unemployed, and on the internet, had led him to Sarah Dillon's call to arms.

"Mike, ready?"

Jenna's green eyes were wide with fear. Not from the exhibits, but at the thought of being caught carrying high-explosives. She was mid-forties, maybe a tad north of that, with dyed black hair and was on a permanent Jewish guilt trip. Mike thought she was wonderful. A self-confessed bored housewife from Seattle, he listened to her diatribes about her dull husband. He sounded a complete prick, especially overlooking a wonderful wife like Jenna.

"Mmm?" Mike couldn't remember what she'd said.

Jenna jerked her head towards the dark pyramid five hundred feet away. Strategic spotlights around the park reflected from polished marble flanks, highlighting the writing carved into the side, a mixture of Egyptian hieroglyphs and Mesopotamian cuneiform. All designed to arouse uneasy feelings. Generating a sense that something slept within that should not be disturbed.

That part was right.

The new phantom had generated headlines around the world as people read about the implications of exactly *what* had been caught. The park played every rumor for maximum publicity, but they had been highly secretive about the nature of the phantom itself. Only that in a classification system that ran from one to five, scientists had been forced to create a sixth tier just for it.

Of course, nobody in the liberation team thought that was anything other than a PR spin for the new multi-million-dollar exhibit.

Mike had to stop himself from running towards the service gate that would allow them backdoor access to the new exhibit. Driven in part by his hatred for the Satori Institute, but mostly to combat the overwhelming sense of dread he was experiencing as they approached the Enclave.

What the hell was in there?

He focused on walking nonchalantly, ignored by the crowds of tourists around them who were more interested in taking selfies than lowly maintenance workers.

They reached the gate when a voice barked at them from behind.

"What're you doing here?"

Mike saw Jenna flinch and hoped the security guard stopping them hadn't noticed. The man was almost as large as Mike and cut a fine figure in the park's stylish security uniform. However, the shock baton, nightstick, and Beretta hanging from his belt reminded him that security here had a formidable reputation. Many a protestor had reported being beaten and shocked for daring to unfold a placard.

"Maintenance. There's a bloody leak in the coolant system."

The guard's eyes narrowed with suspicion. "I didn't hear any report about that."

"Just happened," said Jenna.

"And you arrived like that?" The guard snapped the fingers on one hand, while his other subtly hovered over his belt. With so many VIPs, guests and valuable exhibits, Dillon had warned them that security would be heightened to hair-trigger levels.

"We were already fixing a broken bog," Mike said as casually as he could, even though his heart was beating furiously. "So they asked us. If you like, we'll come back tomorrow." He nodded towards the Enclave. "That place is making me sick."

That seemed to placate the guard. He gave a nod to the door, indicating they should open it. Jenna's hands were trembling as she moved the card to the scanner. The cloned cards had worked so far, but the Enclave posed another level of security. If it were to fail now…

"Your hand's shaking like crazy," the guard noted.

Mike tensed. Armed or not, he'd slug the man if he tried to stop them.

"That's how I've been feeling all evening," said the guard with a laugh. But any humor was lost in seconds as he pointed to the Enclave. "That bastard in there… he just pumps it out."

"Pumps what out?" Mike said with a frown.

"Fear." He raised a hand. It was trembling. "See? Nuts, huh? They've installed some kind of electronic dampers to lessen the effect, but since it arrived, I've hated patrolling this area. There's a thirty-minute limit on workers staying in there too, but they don't care about us little guys walking around outside."

"Bloody corporations," Mike spat. "They only care about the balance sheet."

The guard nodded. "I hear you, brother. I tell you, I don't envy you guys going in there."

Jenna's key card beeped, and the door clicked open. The guard gave a nod of encouragement as they entered.

The bland gray access corridor was nothing special. They could have been in the guts of any public building. It was a straight run that would take them into the exhibit at the heart of the pyramid. However, for the sake of the security cameras, they slowly strolled along and made a pretense of examining the air conditioning conduits overhead. They finally reached the door at the far end and opened it with another swipe of their spoofed key.

A pulsing purple light barely penetrated the darkness beyond. It came from an enormous Tesla shield, the biggest they'd seen in the park. A tram was just edging out of the exhibition hall. They had exactly one minute before the next one would arrive.

The inside of the Enclave was a large spherical space, echoing the black design ethos outside. In the middle was a massive cylindrical tank, like something stolen from SeaWorld. At least forty feet high and a hundred across, the reinforced curved Tesla screen rippled with electrical tension. Beyond, a large black mist swirled. For a new key exhibit, it was massively underwhelming.

The air was thick and humid. Mike was already sweating as he and Jenna parted ways and headed straight for the junction boxes at either end of the enclosure. With every step, Mike's uneasiness grew, coupled with a new sense that he wasn't welcome. The hairs on his arm shot to attention and an inner voice told him to get out as quickly as possible.

They kept to the shadows against the wall. The multiple cameras in the room were focused on the exhibit, leaving plenty of blind spots for them to navigate through.

His hands were shaking when he pried the panel from an electrical junction box, and he shoved a small lump of plastic explosive inside. It wasn't much, just enough to fry the circuits. Zane and Derek had instructed the team on carefully placing the charges to maximize damage. They'd practiced relentlessly, with Zane critiquing every mistake. Yelling at them that rushing it could result in them blowing their own hands off. Mike had appreciated the attention to detail, but right now, the need to leave was almost overpowering, and he felt himself worrying. He hastily inserted the timer and activated it.

The thing in the tank swirled as the dark mass moving in his direction. Details behind the opaque screen were mercifully hidden, but he had the distinct impression that it was studying him.

And whispering…

He looked around to see if there was any other source for the faint chattering. It was as if somebody had left a radio on in another room. He shook his head, but it continued.

He found his concentration meandering. Perhaps the timer should be set a little earlier…?

No. Zane had set them all to go off in a specific sequence. That was important… although he couldn't recall why. His head felt mussy. What would the harm be if he set the timer earlier? Surely that would mean he could leave earlier…

And getting away from here was becoming increasingly desirable…

He twisted the timing dial, watching the clock on the tiny LCD screen roll back. That better...

And maybe… maybe he should check on the others. Just in case…?

Chapter 10

Blake paced the control room, but his eyes never left the screens.

"Checksums are all a-okay," Hugh Pine reported, making his British accent more pronounced, much to everybody's amusement.

For the last two hours, they'd all been on edge since the first tram entered the Enclave, but everything was running like clockwork. Dozens of trams had passed through the new exhibit, with nothing going wrong. Sophie monitored the Raudive levels as they increased when the guests passed through. She had experienced the whispering voice when she'd been close to that *thing*, but the beast never had such a large audience before. Researchers would have a field day with this new behavioral data. Liaising with them was the part of the job she enjoyed the most.

Blake stopped pacing. "Tanaka, any incidents?"

Tanaka swirled his can of Pepsi as he read through the list on his screen. "Two missing children, both reunited. Thirty-six faintings, all minor," that was always the highest accident rate in the park, and one they were proud of. "And a broken tram, but the backup has already taken over."

Blake let out a snort of amazement. The amount of planning that had gone into today had been exceptional, and it looked as if it had paid off. He glanced around when somebody entered the control room.

"Wes! Didn't think I'd see you tonight!" Blake beamed at Wes. He was one of the few ground crew he really appreciated.

"I got splashed, so had to swing by to clean up and get a new uniform." Wes indicated to his freshly laundered clothing. His eyes scanned the screens. "How's it going?"

"Fine. Hey, I wanted to pick your brain about the Wraith Paddock. They've stopped charging the fence. How did you manage that?"

"Oh, easy. The mesh fence they were chewing through, I just upped the harmonics by two thousand hertz." He shrugged as if it was obvious. "Just enough to irritate them, like an itch that won't quit. So now they don't go near it."

"I had the tech team on that for a month!"

"You should've asked me earlier."

"You're wasted, Wes."

"Tell me about it…" Wes muttered, then pointed to a screen. "Is that Elwood's tram heading towards the Enclave?"

"Sure is," said Sophie. "You'll enjoy this. He really hates going in there."

"Can you blame him?" Tanaka shivered in his chair. "I've been in once. Never again."

"Can we watch?" Wes caught Blake's frown. "I have friends on it. I want to see their reaction."

Blake nodded and called up the security cameras. "One of those friends wouldn't happen to be a woman, would it?"

"They're at the Wight Paddock," Sophie said as the tram positioned itself on the entry ramp. "The Enclave is the next stop. Oh, and it's your favorite driver." She looked sidelong at Blake. "Kirk."

Blake harrumphed. "That's what we don't need, two showboaters on one tram."

"Where the hell have you been?" Dillon snapped, barely keeping to a whisper. Her fingers dug into Jenna's elbow as she pulled her closer. She looked furtively around the food plaza to check she hadn't been overheard.

"I was looking for Mike!" Jenna hissed, twisting her arm free from Dillon's grip. The two women had never got on. Jenna had once muttered something about *clashing social circles*. Only their mutual dedication to the cause kept them together. That Jenna had found the enigmatic Welshman quite attractive had made her stick it out far longer than she had intended.

"He's supposed to stay with you. We said don't split up."

"I know! I was finishing in the Enclave when he ran out." She shuddered at the memory. Although she couldn't see the phantom behind the screen, it had made its presence know. A dark, brooding aura of despair had filled her soul. It was worse than being with her husband. Happiness had become a memory, and with every passing second, she felt herself pulled towards the lip of despair…

"What do you mean, ran out?"

She looked around furtively. "You don't know what it was like in there. It was horrible. Like…" She didn't know why she was defending Mike. She was furious that he'd abandoned her.

"What about his…" Dillon looked around and expanded the fingers on one hand to emulate an explosion. She could resist a low accompanying sound effect.

"I checked. They're in place. I suppose he freaked out."

Dillon drew in a sharp breath. She had been worried the pair had been caught, which could have severely compromised the plan. Now it seemed Mike had just let the park get into his head. She checked the WhatsApp group. All the teams had checked in. Mike was the only member missing, but she guessed he was probably halfway out of the park by now.

"Good." She felt herself calm. "Mission accomplished."

Lisa's mind wondered on the journey through the Wight Paddock. She had watched the peculiar creatures, an unholy combination of an equine gorilla, sporting long curved beaks, but Tobias Elwood's commentary washed over her. Her mind strayed to Wes, covered in ectoplasm and with a shovel in his hand. If he was Elwood's superior, then why was he mucking in with the rest of the maintenance crew?

She glanced at Elwood. Appreciating his physique, those smoldering eyes. A rich TV star who traveled the world and faced danger head on. The very definition of a *real* man. She berated herself; she sounded smitten.

Her thoughts drifted to Clarkson and the Chinese party at the front of the tram. Charles Lei's smile had incremented with each exhibit, and his body language towards her boss had thawed considerable. This act of bonding was exactly what they needed to secure the deal. That guaranteed the bonus she needed to cover the financial hole left by many missed maintenance payments. It also meant she was stuck in Vegas for another few years in a job she hated.

And if it wasn't for Wes, they wouldn't be here. That made her angry, although she knew she should be thankful. God, why was she feeling so conflicted? After all, he was just a neighbor. A good friend who'd been there dozens of times when she needed a helping hand, shoulder to cry on, a patient listener to bitch to, or the kids needed looking after. But he was nothing more than a friend. He gave no signs he was interested, or made no moves…

The tram gave a gentle jolt as rolled into a new section. She snapped back to the massive pyramid towering above them, etched in occult runes. She had seen the commercials and listened to Sean and Emma endlessly talk about this place. In real life, it conveyed a tangible sense of dread.

"Welcome to the Enclave," said Elwood, his voice dropping to a fearful whisper that Lisa doubted was an act. "We had five classes of phantoms, as you have seen. From the lowly puddings we first saw, through to the specters. For a while we thought they were as bad as the pans got. Then we discovered that every legend has a basis in fact. Our ancient ancestors didn't fear the unknown. Oh no. They knew *exactly* what to fear. That's when we identified our latest guest and had to create a sixth class of phantom."

As they edged closer, Lisa experienced a tangible ripple of fear.

"If you remember, we use Tesla nets to ensnare Specters and electro-bolas for Wraiths. For each creature, we had to develop new technologies to capture them. Vapos work well on most spooks, especially phantoms, but on this guy, they barely made a dent. We had to pull something special out of the bag for this fella. Major vapo artillery. Catch the parade later and you'll see the new one point eight-terawatt Ion stream vaporizer mounted on an armored car. That's new tech. We didn't have it to bring this guy down. Instead, it took six of us. Poor Taylor..." he added in a low voice. Her obituary had been a footnote to the capture of this new terror.

The tram edged up the entrance ramp towards a huge stone door that was permanently open, revealing Stygian darkness beyond. They didn't need to shut. Nobody would accidentally wonder into this place.

Lisa watched Sean turn towards her, beaming a smile she hadn't seen for such a long time. He gave her the thumbs-up as they entered the Enclave. He was living his dream.

Elwood drew in a breath. "What you are about to experience will push the envelope of fear. Hold tight. And pray to whatever God you have."

Within seconds they were sheathed in a darkness so intense Lisa couldn't see her hand in front of her face. A stale, warm breeze tousled her hair, like a giant breathing. There was nothing obviously alarming, but a shiver ran through her. Voices just on the cusp of legibility began whispering from every direction.

"Since the dawn of humanity, we have feared the darkness. Feared the unknown. Feared our own mortality." Elwood's voice shook with emotion.

A faint illumination rose, revealing a circular tunnel covered in a macabre array of devil's faces and twisted cloaked figures. Recessed holes contained Roman and Medieval death masks. Others displayed Mayan, Chinese, and African burial artefacts.

"Humanity has always searched for ceremonies and trinkets to ward off the unknown. Especially the biggest unknown of them all..."

The walls seemed to rotate around them, giving a disconcerting sensation that they were moving in a spiral towards a black hole.

"Every culture on earth has a legend or superstition concerning death. That is what we all fear the most. The inevitable."

Stone effigies of twisted ancient deities rose from the floor. Lisa didn't know them all, but a few looked familiar from the books the kids had tried to show her and, as an irrational sense of angst rose within her, she wondered what kind of bad parent let their young kids read so much about *death*.

"Azrael, Samael, the Aztec's Xipe Totec, the Egyptian's Anubis and the West's very own Grim Reaper," a stone reaper rotated upwards from the floor, its hand curled around a scythe. "All manifestations of death... and all very real. Mere physical forms of.... *The Angel of Death*."

A darkness smothered them so suddenly that Lisa swore she could feel it. Her ears felt muffled, as if waterlogged. The whispering intensified, as did the urge to flee, coupled with a rank despair that chilled her blood.

Then a huge, curved energy screen appeared along the

length of the tram, and she was aware they had stopped. The sheer folly of parking in some place so awful seemed insane. Something flew beyond the enormous screen. A huge black cloud some twenty-five feet long. It was difficult to make out any detail, as it looked like an inkblot suspended in water.

"The Angle of Death was believed to be nothing more than folklore... until researchers at the Satori Institute discovered this. Phantom royalty."

Everybody shifted in their seats for a better view. In the faint purple glow, she couldn't see Sean and Emma, and had a strong maternal urge to leap from her seat to protect them.

"We call it the Reaper" The bravado in Elwood's voice was replaced with humble respect. Lisa could just see that he was as awestruck as they all were. "The whispering you hear is not a sound effect. It's that thing trying to get into your heads."

Everybody suddenly jumped as the Reaper slammed into the screen with a dull boom.

"Exposure for more than thirty minutes can drive you insane. We had construction workers commit suicide because of it. But don't worry, we have audio-dampers reducing what you hear. It's called a Raudive voice."

The Reaper stopped swirling and hung stationary. As if eying new prey. It was unsettling, and it threw Elwood off his narration.

"Right now your skin is crawling. That is the Reaper stimulating raw fear, which our bodies are responding to. As you can feel, this is stronger than anything you've experienced outside. Our pulse quickens, hearts beat faster, and hormones are dumped. Like the others, it's feeding off our fear. If the others are like small vacuum cleaners. This guy is a black hole."

Lisa closed her eyes. She had broken into an uncomfortable sweat and wondered why anybody would want to pay for such a sickening experience.

"He's approaching limits," Sophie said with concern. Her eyes flicking between the video stream and the readouts on her screen. Kirk would soon receive an alert on his dash instructing him to move out, but she guessed he was already itching to do that. Exposure was a carefully calculated procedure that had to factor in the guests being forced to leave on foot if there was a mechanical failure.

On cue, the tram pulled away.

Wes realized he had been holding his breath during the whole encounter. He'd braved the Enclave several times to get a clearer view of the Reaper, but each time fear and nausea had got the better of him.

"There we go," Blake said with a smile. "Another group of terrified guests." He indicated to a gauge on the screen that had risen from blue to deep red. The PK meter measured the collective hormonal levels secreted by the guests. "Fear levels ran high on that. There are an awful lot of brown trousers in there."

"Yeah, mostly Elwood's," Wes snarked.

Several bright flashes suddenly burst across multiple camera images, like flashbulbs. A second later, the cameras in the Enclave cut to black.

"What the hell?" Blake looked around in alarm as every

other camera across the board suddenly went down en masse.

Then the screens dimmed, and the command center sank into darkness.

The power had been cut.

Tobias Elwood had forged a wildly successful career on the back of being average. A military tour in the marines saw him quickly removed from any frontline engagements, followed by a dishonorable discharge. Naturally, this wasn't on his Wikipedia.

As the atmospheric lights in the Enclave cut out, the only illumination was provided by the Tesla screen throbbing in-and-out of phase. His first instinct was to run. It took every ounce of willpower to keep him glued to his seat. The murmurs of consternation rippling through the carriages were tinged with the belief that this was just another routine scare.

"Not to worry folks, just gremlins in the power." *Christ, I'm a good actor*, he thought. His voice was so firm and calm that he almost convinced himself he had some integrity left. He twisted in his seat and met Kirk's gaze. He was bathed in illumination from the dashboard screens. "What the fuck is going on?" he whispered.

"You can't say that word!" gasped the little girl sitting shotgun. He'd forgotten the kids were there. Not that he didn't like kids, they had made him rich. He just didn't like *other* people's kids. And he had none himself, which was how he intended to continue for the foreseeable.

Kirk jabbed a button. "The Wi-Fi is down. Coms are down." The screen showing the position of the trams around the park now had a single banner across it: signal lost. "It's a Zero Outage." Kirk's voice was low and calm, but the words carried weight.

A pulse of sparks from the Tesla screen suddenly illuminated the chamber and made everybody scream. The Reaper had charged towards them – only to be caught at the last moment by the faint Tesla screen. Ripples of plasma crackled around the shapeless mass as it thrust long clawed fingers through the energy barrier. The screen pulsed, resisting the beast – but then the hands continued pushing through. Each finger was ebony black and a good foot long, crowned by a serrated talon that probed for the humans. Its very touch would decay flesh so rapidly a human would disintegrate in a cloud of blackened ash in seconds. Elwood tried to raise a warning, but his voice caught in his dry throat.

A hiss of voices suddenly infiltrated everybody's consciousness. The Raudive dampers were offline.

Some guests clamped hands over their ears, but that didn't stop the insidious voice. A sibilant rasping combed the language center of the brain, transforming into a disjoined form of whatever the victim's native tongue was. Some vowels sounded in reverse and other words were strung together as a mishmash. The overall effect was deeply unsettling. At the same time, the occupants of the tram heard in both Mandarin and English:

"Frrrreee meee…"

Then the emergency lights suddenly snapped back on. A power surge shot through the Tesla screen. It glowed with a flourish and the clawed hand snapped back into the virtual cage. The voice faded with the faint remnants of a screech that seemed to echo from the back of the skull.

A ripple of embarrassed laughter brought Elwood's focus back to his charges. He forced a jovial chuckle.

"Alright folks, and there you have the Reaper up close and personal. The physical embodiment of death. There is a lot we don't know, like that voice you all heard—"

"I read it talks to other phantoms. Tells them what to do!"

Elwood glanced at the annoying boy behind him and forced a smile. "That's right, kiddo. There's a theory that it uses this to communicate with other phantoms. It's anecdotal, because none of the other pan-species seemed to talk to one another, but we have seen evidence the Reaper does signal to the others. Whether it's language or some sort of base animal communication, we don't yet know, but we think—"

"And it's believed to be ancient Aramaic." The kid clutched his book and beamed with pride.

"Yeah. From *Aramaya*. Nice place. You should go on vacation there." The kid was about to correct him, but Elwood blanked him and put a meaty palm on Kirk's shoulder and whispered. "Kirk, get us the hell out of here. Fast." Kirk didn't need asking twice. His foot was already on the pedal.

"Say goodbye to the park's latest star. You'll be having nightmares about him for the rest of the month!"

Elwood knew that experience would hound him for the rest of the year. He made a vow to avoid the Enclave in the future. Trapping the bastard in Egypt had been an encounter he had no wish to ever repeat.

Chapter 11

Running from the super-chilled air-conditioned control hub into the dry desert was like running into soup. Wes stopped to soak in the moment. The lights were on in the avenues, although a couple of stores had plunged into darkness. The power cut had not been complete, thank god. The emergency lighting in the hub had come online, but the cameras were still down.

He was moving on autopilot with the sole idea of helping Elwood. Or rather, Lisa and the kids. His mobile was down, as was the park's Wi-Fi, so Calvin couldn't coordinate his team. At least Wes wouldn't be missed. On his way out of the hub, Steinberg had tossed him a walkie-talkie that was picking up chatter from the security team. By the time he sprinted to a spare golf cart and stamped the foot brake, the emergency generators had absorbed the load, and everything seemed to be back to normal.

Exactly as had been designed.

Wes felt a glimmer of relief. The park had never experienced power issues before, although they had rehearsed such emergency drills endlessly and every member of staff was trained in using vapos, Tesla nets and other tools needed to stupefy and subdue the exhibits. Not that any of them had any *real* experience in it.

He floored the pedal, pushing the vehicle to a heady twelve miles per hour as he cut down Main Street. All the guests appeared relaxed and lost in the experience, assuming any bangs they heard were part of an attraction. Only the telltale signs of something significantly wrong were the occasional shops or coffee stores without power. That, and the constant chatter on his radio. It was difficult to pick out a common thread, but there appeared to be several sightings of smoke from substations around the park, and suspicions were pointed at a potential overload being the cause. That made sense. The park was running at peak performance and the new exhibits that had been added since opening day definitely strained the system. The Enclave itself hogged a huge amount of power.

The throngs of people cutting across his path kept forcing him to tap the brake. Wes knew he'd move faster on foot, but the heat would sap his strength in minutes. He jinked the wheel to the left, narrowly avoiding a family posing for selfies in the middle of the road. He yelled a company approved apology but kept straight on down the branching street.

Ahead, he saw the tip of the Enclave pyramid and, alarmingly, the definite shade of black smoke against the night sky. Crossing over his path ahead was the electromagnetic monorail. Normally the quickest way to shuttle around the park, now the train was beached on the track after losing power. He saw fleeting glimpses of the panicking passengers trapped inside, before he passed under it.

To the right, he glimpsed smoke rising from a nearby

utility area. He knew one substation was there. He unhooked the radio from his belt to report it – when he caught a sudden orange flash, followed seconds later by a sharp snap. Nothing dramatic. It was small, like the premature opening of a fireworks display.

Two figures sprinted away. Their furtive movements clearly signs that they were not panicking guests, and definitely not staff.

Wes was so fixated he failed to notice he was drifting to the side of the road until the wheels hit the fake black grass and he smashed into a lamppost.

"What the hell is going on?" hissed Zane as he watched the fireball erupt from the substation behind them.

"You must've set the timer wrong!" shriek Anna, her heart thumping in her chest. This was the first time she had actually entered the park after sharing her loathing and criticism from the safety afforded by Twitter. Now she was here, her disgust about the poor caged creatures had faltered. They were ugly and weird enough to be destroyed. They were not meant for this world.

"I know how to handle a charge," Zane growled. "The timer was fine. I double checked all of them."

"Maybe they're faulty?" Anna winced, her hand shooting to her ear as a sequel of tinnitus from the explosion suddenly gave way to a hiss, like static. Amongst it, the vaguest of voices seemed to pop and whine, *almost* forming words. "What is that?"

Zane winced too, although from his expression it wasn't as irritating as she found it. Then he did a double take.

"What's Mike doing here?"

She followed his gaze to see Mike moving at a rapid pace away from them. In the streetlights, she could see the sheen of sweat covering his face as if he had been running a marathon. He didn't look back at the premature explosion, or at the golf cart that had careened from the road just seconds ago.

"He was supposed to go from the Enclave to the east side," said Zane, shaking his head as the whispering static faded away. Something was wrong. After a shared look, they followed him.

Ahead, Mike stumbled as if exhausted, but quickly recovered himself and shouldered through a bunch of guests who bleated their disapproval. Mike ignored them, no longer playing the charade of a maintenance guy. He was driven by a higher calling.

The street opened up on one side to a wide spacious enclosure decorated with ancient burial mounds and more contemporary graves from a swathe of religions. It was the Wight Paddock. The six huge bull-like beasts walked on all-fours, their triple-hinged forelimbs gouging the ground to dig up graves. Their front legs were longer than the rear, giving them an odd ape-like stance. Their long beaked heads were designed to feast on the exposed corpses in the ground, or in this case, the rotten meat buried to feed them. At least fifty people stood at the tesla-screen, recording the wights on their phones. They also captured the moment the Tesla security screen fizzled and extinguished as it lost power.

Being subtly opaque, only a few of the guests noticed the power loss. But the wights did. Heads snapped up as they sensed the painful barrier that had hemmed them in was no more. With a sudden rush of speed, they charged the crowd.

Murmurs rose, but most guests had seen such bravado displays from the other spooks in the park. A critter smashing against the screen as it tried to devour you, had become a badge of honor.

Screams only erupted when the first wight bounded over the low metal perimeter wall that housed the Tesla-tech. It trampled four people underfoot before they could react. The snapping of bones was drowned out, first by the screams erupting in the crowd, and then by the haunting hoot of the creature itself, as it smelled fresh blood for the first time in over a year.

"This is bad!" cried Anna as she watched the panic unfold.

The trampled victims were hurled to the floor. They reached out for help – but and nobody was brave enough to assist. Instead, bystanders fled. In the chaos, Anna lost sight of Mike.

Zane opened his mouth to speak, but was then struck by a charging wight. Anna froze in terror. The big bull was almost twice her size. Zane was tossed into the air and sent sprawling yards away, breaking a dozen bones as he did. Not content with freedom, the wight pursued its prey. A clawed foot pinned Zane in the back. The monstrous beak snapped forward and effortlessly tore into his flesh.

Anna only pulled her gaze away when she saw Zane's bloodied spine being torn free.

Wes shook his head to clear his senses. He'd struck the post barely at a run, but his head hit the wheel hard and knocked him out for a couple of seconds. *Idiot*, he chided himself. A wave of screams made him look around. While the screams were the park's signature soundtrack, the mass of fleeing wasn't.

"Oh shit," he murmured as the first wight trotted into view, chasing a knot of guests like a cocaine-fueled bull.

His radio suddenly burst into chatter. Conversations overlapping with rising panic: *more explosions, power failing everywhere, Tesla shields falling.*

The streetlights flickered, then died. The darkness was amplified by the wails of terror. He clambered from the cart as the radio chatter continued with increasing levels of panic. He stepped into the street to clear his throbbing head.

"Another explosion! Dozens Dead! Elwood has diverted towards the banshee tunnels!"

The Banshee Tunnels? Did he hear that right? Kirk and Elwood were smart enough to know they needed to stay clear. Didn't they realize the power was out? Perhaps the outage hadn't reached them yet? Lisa and the kids were still on that tram.

There because of *him*.

He turned back to the cart, having aimlessly stepped a few yards into the road just as a wight rumbled out of the darkness and butted the vehicle with its thick skull, mistaking it for a rival. The vehicle rolled onto its roof, which crumpled from the weight. The beast struck it again, forcing the cart end-over-end like a toy.

It was enough of a distraction for Wes to run for his life.

'This can't be right,' said Sean as the tram turned onto a dark street. A chorus of distant confused voices turned to shouts and then a tsunami of screams.

Kirk knew this was more than a minor power outage. Where the hell were the backup generators? Dual lines of protection should have kicked in by now. His foot hovered over the brake, but the thought of stopping in the darkness held little appeal. He recalled the basic rule around here: don't stop in the dark. He felt an urgent tap on his shoulder. Elwood's voice was close to his ear. He couldn't be certain, but was there a trace of fear there?

"Head to the light. Whatever you do, don't stop," Elwood hissed.

Kirk saw the lights of a building to the right. The darkness cast an illusion of misdirection over him, and in a moment of irrationality, he couldn't work out quite where they were in the park.

"Banshee tunnel," Emma read from the map on the tram's control screen. She folded her arms grumpily, oblivious to the alarm circulating through the adults. "I've seen them already!"

Kirk didn't care. Beyond the artificial tree, the subtle

entrance lights beckoned them with a soft purple glow, indicating that the path inside was clear of any other tram. More importantly, it indicated there was still power. His dramatic mashing of the pedal produced barely an imperceptible amount of acceleration. Screams continued in the darkness behind. Not those of fright, but wet and agonized ones. Kirk glanced over his shoulder but saw nothing other than Elwood gripping onto a pole and staring into the darkness with an ashen face.

"Don't stop!" Elwood said in barely a whisper.

Kirk aimed straight for the center of the archway, plummeting into the darkness beyond. He knew he should come to a stop and allow the moving track to carry them in a lazy-S through the landscape, but the desire to put distance between him and the outside world was overwhelming.

The tram wheels caught on the recessed guides in the floor, removing the need for steering. The steering wheel gently turned in his hands as he powered forward into the darkness. The faintest of lights on the ground, concealed from the passengers, assured him there was power, but the track wasn't moving. His anxiety was suddenly spiked when they passed the first sensor that triggered the lightning effects. Nothing happened, and the huge panoramic LED screens illuminated with a dim glow rather than their full 8K resolution.

Kirk glanced at the control panel, then at Sean next to him. "Something's not—"

"Look out!" Sean pointed ahead – but it was too late to stop.

Another tram was blocking the track. Kirk slammed into the back of it with the velocity of a funfair dodgem. It was enough to jerk him hard against the steering wheel and toss Sean from the side of the cab as they came to a halt.

Consternation rose behind him. Elwood twisted around to see what had happened.

"Everybody okay?" Elwood called out, but he wasn't paying attention to the answers. "Oh, shit…" his gaze was fixed ahead.

Everybody's eyes were adapting to the darkness. The screens were pumping out just enough illumination to see the farmhouse and trees, as if bathed in the faintest moonlight. The white tram ahead was empty and covered in black stains. Liquid dripped from the car's covered ceiling. Elwood slowly stood for a better view. The carriages were littered with headless corpses, the darkness mercifully masking gruesome details.

Then he realized the faint glow from the Tesla tunnel walls was not there. The shields were down.

"Here they come!" Emma pointed as two dark shapes zigzagging to the right of the tram as they slowly circled towards the new victims.

Elwood's blood ran cold. "Everybody cover your ears!"

Kirk couldn't release his iron grip on the steering wheel as he watched the banshees drift closer, just as he'd seen them do many times before. Only then did he remember that this was a distraction technique they employed when attempting an ambush.

He slowly turned to see a third banshee suspended from the canopy of the carriage in front. It silently dropped on the hood of his tram. He'd never seen them so close. Even in the twilight, he could make out the skin as rough as sandpaper; the black holes that served as eyes; and the hyperextending mouth.

Then it screamed.

Elwood had his hands clamped across his ears, but even so, the banshee's wail felt like somebody was shoving needles into his eardrums. Emma, crouched alongside Kirk, had done the same, as well as screwing up her eyes and looking away. Which was fortunate.

Kirk still gripped the wheel, fixated on the black opening mouth. Viscous fluid oozed from the maw, and he was overpowered by the stench of carrion. Then it unleashed a sonic scream.

The flesh on Kirk's face rippled as if caught in a jet stream. His ear drums perforated instantly, but the scream continued to resonate through his head as a deep rumble. Capillaries across his forehead and cheeks swelled and ruptured. His eyeballs burst like wet sacs. The epidermis, fat layer and hair were blasted away. Muscles were raked and shredded seconds later. His brain liquified and dribbled from his nose. The integrity of his skull became as frail as an eggshell. In four seconds Kirk's head imploded, spraying blood and brain matter across a stunned Elwood and a curled-up Emma. Kirk's corpse toppled from the car inches from where Sean still lay, flat on his back on the Irish diorama.

The banshee spotted the prone boy. Hunched on its forearms, it stalked forward.

Elwood was paralyzed with fear, aware that, in the carriages behind him, the guests were all out of their seats, hesitating whether to stay put or jump. The pair of circling banshees now swooped in, landing on the canopy above their heads. The clatter of claws on metal marked their movements towards the edge.

"Do something!" yelled Clarkson, pushing the Chinese translator as a barrier between him and the open side of the cart.

Lisa scrambled forward, clambering over the bench

seats. She had watched Kirk's fate from a distance. It hadn't been far enough.

"EMMA! SEAN!"

Then she saw the creature that had killed Kirk was crawling across the front of the tram towards Sean, who was sprawled on his back, legs kicking as he put distance between him and the creature.

He hadn't seen the fourth banshee creeping up from behind. She grabbed Clarkson's shoulder and pointed.

"Help me!"

Her boss gave a stricken look – then his gaze switched to something *behind* her. She spun to see a banshee head poking down from the canopy. Its mouth gaped. Lisa covered her ears and dropped to the floor as the sonic blast was unleashed.

Blood splattered her. She looked up to see Charles Lei had been standing behind her and taken the full blast. His head had imploded, yet his body was still standing, jerking as his nervous system fired off. His translator next to him howled in despair–

Then claws suddenly plucked her from behind, dragging her out of the tram. Lisa reached for her kicking feet, but the woman was taken too quickly. Clarkson did not help. He watched, open-mouthed, as the banshee carried the screaming woman over the artificial landscape. Another swooped in, and she was tossed in the air between them, limbs flailing as she was caught and thrown again – before being dropped to the ground. She tried to stand on a broken leg, but only limped a couple of steps before the pair of banshees dive-bombed her. Her screams became wet, then stopped.

Lisa was operating on autopilot. She barged past Clarkson. Ahead, Elwood was frozen in place, hands over his ears and his face spattered in gore. Mofa Quantum's CFO blocked her path as he cowered behind the bench seat. He reached out to pull her for cover, but she slipped from his grasp and leaped from the side. She landed on the hard grass hillock that sloped up from the tram track and turned into the fake corn lining the enclosure's perimeter.

She reached for her son. "Sean! Behind!"

He was inching backwards, but with an expression of wonder rather than one of terror. With a sibilant hiss, the banshee extended its mouth—

The roar of a gas engine howled as a park jeep ramped over the sculpted mound. The creature squealed as the vehicle slammed it hard into the side of the tram. The banshee Sean had been backing towards suddenly took to the air in fright.

Smoke rose from the crumpled hood as the engine stalled. The banshee was stuck fast, claws raking the metal as it struggled to release itself. But it wasn't dead; it would take more than *that* to kill it.

It wailed. The sonic blast imploded the windshield over the driver.

Lisa saw it was Wes. He was wearing protective goggles and yellow ear defenders. His forearms were raised to deflect the flurry of glass. Then he heaved a vapo inside the jeep's cramped cab and fired through the windshield.

The ion volley crackled, searing the vehicle's paintwork as it struck the trapped creature. Ripples flowed through its body seconds before it exploded in a mass of purple and green gunk.

Wes staggered from the jeep, the vapo propped over one shoulder as he helped Sean up.

"Are you okay?"

Sean nodded excitedly. "That was amazing!" He obviously hadn't witnessed the blood and gore.

Lisa ran to them, hugging Sean tightly and repressing a sob.

"Are you hurt? Are you okay?"

Sean tried to break her grip as he seethed with embarrassment. "I'm alright, mom."

Wes spotted the remaining three banshees circling them, ready to swoop. He reached into a bag on the jeep's passenger seat and tossed them a pair of ear defenders.

"Put them on."

The Bose defenders not only muffled the ambient noise around them, but these were also specially made to cancel out the banshee's bespoke wailing. He took the bag and whistled at Elwood – who didn't respond as he was still covering his ears. Too late, Wes tossed the bag. It whacked the big man on the side of the head. He flinched, then looked at Wes in surprise.

"West?"

He reached for the bag – just as a banshee landed on the side of the tram, causing the carriage to rock. It spread its mouth wide. Wes swung the vapo – but fumbled. It dropped to the floor.

With a grunt, Elwood punched the banshee across the head. It was hard enough to knock the beast from the side of the tram. Elwood plucked the ear defenders from the bag – and put them on as the banshee screamed at him. The impact felt as if he'd run face-first into a wind tunnel, but without the harmful harmonic accompaniment, he only felt a few capillaries in his face swell and burn. He silenced the beast with another punch, then jumped from the tram and retrieved Wes' vapo.

"Time to fry, asshole!" he yelled – not that he could hear himself.

A single cool, measured blast burst the banshee apart like a wet bag of trash.

Lisa ran into the tram cab, desperately trying not to look at Kirk's beheaded remains. Emma was still curled up, head between her knees and forearms clamped across her ears. She was covered in blood. Lisa shoved a pair of ear defenders on her, then scooped her up, making sure she couldn't see the death around them.

Wes gestured for the others to follow him back the way he came, through the Banshee Tunnel exit. Mofa Quantum's CFO broke for cover, yelling in Mandarin – a mistake that caught the banshees' attention. One swooped in – plucking the man backwards, dragging him into the artificial field. There was a rending of flesh and bone. Then he fell silent.

Elwood took potshots at the remaining banshee, but it kept its distance. Clarkson was shouting, gesturing at Elwood and punching the air. Everything lost in the defender's noise cancellation. He asserted himself and took the lead, his weapon ready to fire at the slightest provocation.

Wes hesitated. Glancing back at his friend's body. Grief would have to wait. Now it was all about survival.

Chapter 12

Dillon and Kyle crouched in the darkness behind a hot dog stall. The air was ripe with the continuous anguish of sixty thousand people. The Transylvanian plaza in front of them was littered with carcasses, injuries hidden by the darkness. A souvenir store directly across from them was ablaze, the glow reflecting from a flock of circling imps. They landed on a street lamp, which they began to gnaw.

People occasionally raced past – couples, families, or bleeding and confused employees. A gibbering phantom swooped in pursuit of an overweight man in a hideous Hawaiian shirt and shorts. Slender arms sliced through the back of his shirt. Dillon noticed the phantom wasn't rushing to catch up with its prey. It was satisfied by feeding from the man's fear, not flesh. It would toy with him until he died of exhaustion.

"This is sabotage," Dillon said under her breath. She was torn between elation at seeing the creatures freed and shock by the death she was witnessing.

"Who'd sabotage us?"

Dillon shook her head. "Do you remember the map?"

They had blindly fled down streets to avoid the hordes of creatures pouring from confinement. The darkness had further compounded their disorientation when they stumbled across the faux Transylvanian architecture straight from old Universal B-movies.

"We're central." Kyle indicated down an avenue opposite. "I think that's the route to the parking lots."

Dillon stood, but kept hunched over. "Let's make a run for it. Come on!"

She took several steps – before a hideous specter burst from the burning store. It was twice her size. Purple skin looked shredded and was difficult to focus on, part of its optical camouflage. Black slashed eyes narrowed as it fixed on her. This was an African variant, a pure carnivore. Its mouth widened into a grimace, exposing hundreds of hooked teeth. They curved backwards, pulling prey into its mouth and never letting go. Its arms were long and thin, but exceptionally powerful. It loomed over her in a classic position to strike down.

She was staring death in the face.

Something swung in from the side – a spinning, expanding net. It struck the specter and immediately blazed to life with an electrical current that sizzled the air. With a shriek, the beast dropped to the floor, pawing at the Tesla net.

Her savior was a woman in a park technician's uniform. She looked at Dillon and pointed.

"Get into cover. There's an emergency bunker—"

Her arm was suddenly bitten off by a second specter swooping from above. Blood smattered across Dillon. The stunned technician stared at her stump as the specter circled back for her. She was hoisted off her feet and carried, screaming, into the darkness.

The netted specter snarled. The shock had phased it to become solid, but hadn't killed it. It struggled to get out of the net, teeth gnashing at the tungsten wires.

Dillon flinched as an arm draped around her shoulder. She turned to punch her assailant.

"Whoa!" Kyle held up his other hand. "It's me! Easy!"

He stared at the severed arm on the floor. Then threw up.

Dillon backed from the netted specter as it drew closer. "We need to go."

She led him towards the shadows of the avenue they hoped would lead to freedom.

"Confirmed Zero Outage." Sophie leaned back in her chair, too stunned to say any more.

The control bunker was operating on emergency power. While the systems were back in operation, the cameras and sensors they connected to across the park were dead. They were blind. The only saving grace was the air con still worked.

Blake paced before the screens. The video feeds were blank, but the park schematic was still up, running from local computers. But with no input, it was just a glorified map.

Hugh Pine slapped his keyboard in frustration. "Internet's down!" he looked at his cell phone propped on the desk next to his monitor. "And no mobile reception."

Because of the huge electrical fields flowing around the park, Phantom Land was a signal dead zone. A network of signal booster stations had been installed to provide a basic signal. With the power gone, those towers were useless.

"We've lost contact with the outside world," confirmed Sophie, with a tremor in her voice. "Wes took the only radio with him."

"We might be the ones who are in the dark," Blake suggested optimistically. "If things are still up and running outside, it could be the pipelines into this place are down." He knew it was wishful thinking, but he was clutching at straws.

"Open the door and find out," Tanaka suggested.

They all swapped looks. The walls of the bunker were charged and made from graphene and exotic elements designed to prevent even pan-dimensional entities from drifting through them. If there was something outside, then the moment they opened the door, they lost that advantage.

Ying Yue stood up from her desk. "Mr Blake, sir. I have a radio." She held it up.

Blake motioned for her to hand it over.

"I was checking the security gate earlier," said Ying, "and forgot to hand it back in." She sounded apologetic.

Blake broke into a grin. "All the state-of-the-art tech inside, and you may have just saved us all a lot of worry with an old walkie-talkie."

He turned it on.

At first, they thought it was the squelch and hiss of a bad signal, before they realized they were listening to the constant sound of thousands of people screaming in terror.

Panicked voices cut over one-another in their haste to report.

The Specter Corral is out! No power at the Wight Paddock! They're attacking everybody! Bodies everywhere!

Blake snapped the power off. He grit his teeth and felt a sharp pain in his chest. A heart attack would be a saving grace at this juncture.

"We need to see what's going on out there," said Tanaka.

Blake stared at the pyramid at the center of the giant map.

"No. We need to know what's going on in there. Hugh, reboot everything."

Hugh looked uncertainly at his colleagues. "If we're running on emergency power and turn things off again, there's a chance they might not reboot. We'll lose the systems completely."

Blake gestured to the screen. "We've already lost them. Reboot."

Hugh hesitated, then nodded. He rapidly peeled away the multiple layers of security settings until he reached the core hub controls.

"Are we all ready?"

Blake nodded. Hugh took a deep breath, then tapped a virtual toggle switch.

The lights went out. The air con ground to a halt. Every computer system fell dead.

Nobody spoke for almost forty seconds.

Then a wave of lights rushed across the control desks as screens booted up. Blake exhaled the breath he'd been holding as the park map appeared on the screen. It took a full four minutes for all the systems to come back online, ending with the welcome whirl of the air conditioning.

"Cameras are still down," noted Hugh.

"But we have grid statistics," Sophie yelled with relief.

Across the map, several lines to the east of the park faintly glowed. "Some specter and phantom fences are up. Only just." The dread was building in her voice. "We have seventy percent failure, and it's falling."

Blake swore under his breath. He glanced at the younger technicians, who were watching the map with increasing concern. "I want a full inventory of what might have got out." He was clutching to the hope that they were mostly harmless exhibits, but they had all heard the terror on the radio. His real concern lay at the center of the map.

A purple line slowly faded up around the pyramid. He groaned in relief.

"The Enclave still has power," Tanaka said.

"Thank God for that," muttered Blake.

Tanaka pointed between the dark areas where the fences had gone down, and a set of fluctuating bar graphs to the side. All of them were struggling to stay at mid-level. "These are the original enclosures. They were never designed to compete for power with new systems like the Enclave." When the park had been designed only a few short years ago, even the leading scientists exploring pan-dimensional rifts had never imagined such power demands would be required for a Class VI phantom. "They're all on the same circuit. So the Enclave has basically sucked them dry."

"Thanks to poor planning," Hugh said under his breath.

Blake was only half-listening. He was gauging the distance between the open enclosures to the west and the eastern parking structures. That's where people would flee to. And where there's people, the pans would follow. Some entities were incredibly fast over short distances, like specters, but they all lacked the energy over distances. There was still a chance they hadn't breached the wall.

"Fire up the SkyShield."

Tanaka cracked his knuckles and began accessing the system.

Hugh gave him a nervous look. Blake caught it.

"What?"

Hugh pointed to the energy bars on the side screen. "The SkyShield's power demands override almost everything else. Only the Enclave and this place are kept on separate loops, and both operate on more juice than we currently have. We're running on fumes." He saw Blake didn't get what he was driving at. "With the SkyShield up, we risk deactivating all the remaining security fences that are still functional."

"We'll be unleashing almost everything," Sophie said quietly.

Blake looked grim as he turned back to the screen. His gaze was drawn to the Enclave. "Not everything." The pain in his chest increased, and he absently rubbed the spot, hoping it was nothing more than a muscle cramp. "If we don't, then they'll breach the wall and head to the nearest source of human activity." He looked at everybody in the room. "And that means goodbye Vegas. Activate the shield," he said firmly.

Tanaka nodded and opened the two virtual security panels. He pressed his palm against a scanner to identify himself, then thumbed the large green button.

The lights in the room flickered. Everybody silently watched as the periphery Tesla Towers powered up. And as they did, the lights on the remaining secure paddocks dimmed...

Chapter 13

Lisa pulled her children in either hand as they ran towards a dark ghost themed diner, nestled in an avenue of misshapen trees that looked ready to spring to life and consume them.

Emma hadn't said a word since the Banshee Tunnels, and when Sean noticed the bodies dotted around the streets, his excitement faded.

Elwood led the way, wielding the vapo. Clarkson keeping as close to his hero as possible. Since stepping outside and discarding the ear defenders that made their ears sweat, Clarkson had overlooked Wes' heroic act and heaped nothing but praise on the TV star.

Elwood didn't dare turn around in case they saw the terror on his face that betrayed his inadequacy. Wes brought up the rear, scanning the streets for any threat. With the lights out, he was reassured to see the glow of a security fence behind the diner.

"The power's still on this side of the park," he pointed. "That's the *Deogen* Forest."

Sean spoke up, relieved to have something to fixate on.

"They're the Belgium ghosts, right? They look like fog with eyes."

"You make them sound like something out of Scooby-Doo, kid," Elwood said, also thankful for the distraction. "Those blood-red eyes'll give you nightmares. My camera guy almost lost a leg when–"

They all stopped in the tracks as the sky suddenly lit up. Purple pulses of energy washed overhead, suspended in the darkness and rippling like the Aurora Borealis.

"What's that?" Lisa asked, scooping Emma up in her arms.

"The SkyShield!" Sean was delighted. Few people ever got to see it for real, and most tests were done during the daylight hours when it was almost invisible. Now it danced and rippled, casting a soft pink hue below. It wasn't a replacement for the streetlights, but it helped dispel some shadows.

"What does it do?" said Clarkson, eyeing the new development with uncertainty.

"It stops the exhibits from escaping from the park," Sean said with some authority. He held up the encyclopedia he had salvaged from the tram as they escaped. "You should read this. It's all in here."

"They can't get out?" Lisa asked with some relief.

Elwood cast a dark look at Wes. They both knew what else it meant.

"Neither can we," said Wes quietly.

Everybody looked at him, but he couldn't keep his eyes off the sky. "It was designed to contain a small breakout. Hunter teams would move in and contain the threat. Then they switch it off."

As he spoke, they all noticed the glow from the Deogen Forest was fading to nothing.

"It's leeching the power from everything else." Wes looked at Lisa, telegraphing his concern, but not wanting the children to hear it. "We should find cover. Right now."

They sprinted towards the diner.

Elwood shouldered the door open, his gun sweeping the room. There were no signs of a struggle. Fast-food meals had been left half-eaten on the tables as diners fled. Wes shut the door quietly behind them. The full glass windows overlooking the avenue beyond would offer zero protection from an assault. Then again, neither would a steel wall. It would have to do while they figured out a plan.

The clatter of movement from behind the counter had Elwood spinning around. Next to a long cooking grill, three leathery bat-winged gremlins were attached to the wall, one biting the smooth steel door of a meat locker. Their adhesive limbs held them in place as their necks cracked awkwardly back to peer at the newcomers with round, black eyes.

"Gremlins!" Sean gasped.

Elwood grimaced and pulled the vapo trigger. Wes pushed his arm aside.

"Don't!"

A stream of charged ions shot took a chunk out of a support stanchion close to Clarkson's head and blew out a plate-glass window behind him. The gremlins scattered with a screech, heading straight through the open window.

"What the hell did you do that for, Talaga?" Elwood bellowed.

"They're only gremlins! They damage machines, not people! And it's *Talasky*!" Wes snapped as he strode towards the grill and turned the gas off. "And if the ion stream had struck this, you would've blown us all up!"

Sean gave Elwood a curious look. "They're not poisonous like imps. They're kinda cool."

Elwood pulled a face, but said nothing.

Wes looked at the scratches on the locker door. "They were trying to get in…"

He slowly reached for the handle.

"Talasky, don't!" hissed Elwood.

The latch clunked, and Wes pulled the door open. Elwood raised the vapo, his finger on the trigger. But he checked his fire when three people toppled from the confined space. They wore the diner uniform, two thin teenagers and a burly cook who took most of the space.

"Thank God!" gasped the girl, taking in deep breaths. Her name badge read: Becky "I thought we'd die in there." Her eyes widened when she saw Elwood. "Thank you!" She ran over and flung her arms around him, kissing his cheek.

"You're welcome," said Elwood, cocking his charming grin as the other two staff members – Ralph and Scott - lavished their thanks for him saving them. They all ignored Wes, who was still holding the door open.

"The power went off and then we saw a flock of phantoms pass right through," Ralph, the cook, explained. He poured himself a JD from the small corner bar. He knocked it back and quickly filled the glass again. "The diners ran for their lives. Staff too. We stayed back when the screaming started. Then those gremlins flew in the open door, and we hid in here so they couldn't get us."

"You're safe now," said Elwood, basking in their adoring looks.

Wes looked at him incredulously. "What? We can't stay here!"

"I don't see why not."

"We're sitting ducks. There's no protection. With the SkyShield up, we're trapped in here along with them."

Clarkson stared contemptuously at Wes. "I wouldn't be here if it wasn't for you, Talasky." He wheeled on Lisa, his temper blackening. "And your stupid idea just cost me one of the biggest accounts my agency was likely to see. Lei was going to sign before you got him killed!"

Lisa's lips trembled on the cusp of an outburst, but Clarkson was on a roll. He paced anxiously back and forth, gesturing to Elwood. "And we have a bone fide expert right here, the world expert on all this shit, and you have the audacity to question him?" He stepped close to Wes, leaning into his face. "HA!" spittle struck Wes's cheeks. "Who should I believe? A pumped-up zookeeper or a reality TV star?" He looked at the others as if the choice was obvious. He jabbed a finger in Wes' ribs. "And as soon as we're out of here, I'm going to raise an army of lawyers and sue this place. And specifically, *you*."

It took a few moments for Wes to find his voice. It trembled with fragile confidence.

"You should do what you do best. Good for you. Why don't you sue the animals too? I bet that'll really turn you on." Wes did not know where his courage was coming from; perhaps from the desire to stay alive. He raised his voice to address the others. "I don't know what you think these windows are going to hold back." He gestured to the broken one. "We're even screwed if it rains. The shield will suck up every joule of power. I don't know how many exhibits are loose, but I have no intention of standing around counting them." He addressed Elwood, hoping he could break through the ego. "We need to get everybody to the command hub as quickly as possible. It's the only safe place."

Elwood sipped from an abandoned chocolate shake. "The hub's too far–"

Lisa found her voice. "Listen, Mr Elwood. I know you're the face on TV, but shouldn't you be listening to him?" She put an arm on Wes's shoulder.

"Why would I do that?"

"He's your boss, for one. And for two–"

"My what?" A smirk crossed Elwood's face. "West is my boss?"

"Wes," Wes mumbled as Elwood clamped a huge hand on his other shoulder. "And this isn't really the time–"

"No, no, no," Elwood cajoled. "This is gold, my friend. What have you been telling her?" He lowered his voice, just not enough to prevent everybody from hearing. "You trying to get into her panties or something?"

Ralph couldn't hold back a loud snigger.

"Elwood. Just cool it…"

Elwood lightly flicked Lisa's chin. "Sweetheart. I head-lined three seasons of Spook Hunters. I got a closet filled with Golden Globes, Emmys, and one of those BAFTA things. A ton of other stuff. While Wes here shovels ecto-plasm for a living."

All eyes turned to Wes. He cringed, feeling wretched. He couldn't meet Lisa's look, but accidentally saw Sean peering at him with betrayal.

Elwood continued. "That's right folks, he's a profes-sional shit-shoveler." He lapped up the laughter spent at Wes' expense. "But it's a free country if you want to put your life in his hands…"

Wes noticed there had been a subtle shift in the room's dynamics. People had edged away from him and stepped closer to Elwood's invisible cone of protection. Including Lisa. His face burned with embarrassment. In the silence, he focused back on the screaming outside. He couldn't let this be about him. He sucked in a breath and stepped closer to Elwood. He lowered his voice, hoping the others couldn't hear.

"If we don't find somewhere safe to hide, then you're going to be the headline on TMZ who sat back and offered these people up as a buffet, while you did nothing about it."

That got through to him. Elwood hefted the vapo as he addressed the group.

"Okay, folks. The way I see it is, we can bunker down here and take potshots if any of those things try to come in." He wasn't pleased with the relieved looks being shared, so he quickly continued. "Or we can make a break for it down Terror Boulevard." He gestured westwards along the road outside. Wes inwardly groaned that the meathead had used the street name.

Wes pointed to the north. "It's in that direction…" but nobody was listening as Elwood continued.

"It'll take us straight to the hub." He looked at Clarkson. "That'll be the quickest place for extraction."

Clarkson laughed and nodded. "See? That's proper leadership. Lead the way."

Everybody followed Elwood to the door. Carrying Emma in her arms, Lisa lingered back with Sean. Wes bashfully joined them.

"Are you guys okay?"

Lisa nodded but cast a black look at Clarkson. Sean said nothing and clutched his book across his chest.

"Are we going to die?" Emma whispered. Lisa choked back a sob.

Wes forced a smile. "No. Where would the fun be in that?" He jerked a thumb towards Elwood. "And Elwood's right here. It's like we're on TV. If you look carefully, you might be able to see the TV cameras."

She followed his gaze outside and nodded solemnly. "I think I see them."

"Good. Because one of the rules for being on Spook Hunters is that you've got to appear as brave as possible." He winked.

That seemed to rally her confidence. She jiggled, indicating Lisa should put her down. With Sean, they followed the others out of the diner.

As she passed, Lisa quietly said, "You're quite something, Wes."

Wes was sure it was an insult. What else could it have been?

Where the SkyShield met the park's crenelated perimeter wall, the plasma crackled and popped with such intensity that it resonated through Sarah Dillon's ribcage. The shield extended through the wall, sealing the exit gates to the parking lot.

Some fifty people were clustered around it, nervously watching two college students rolling on the ground. Despite the icon and printed warning: DO NOT CROSS IF SHIELD IS UP, they had tried to run through it, resulting in severe burns. Their hair and skin were smoking where it had come into contact with the high-powered charge.

Some enterprising people had tried to push a souvenir

cart through the glowing curtain, but it was like striking stone. The harder they pushed, the more the wood sizzled and charred until it ignited. Nothing could be seen beyond the opaque screen, and Dillon doubted the crowd's pleas to be released would penetrate it either.

Jenna clung to Kyle, who was still catching his breath from the dash to the gate. "What now?"

They eyed the remaining five wheeled barrow stalls circled the gate to entice visitors into one final purchase: balloons, plastic vapos, books, nothing of any use.

"The shield circles the park." Dillon recalled the intel they had gathered on the park's security features.

"If we follow it around, we might find a hole or something," Kyle said hopefully.

Dillon shook her head. "It's an energy matrix. It doesn't have any *gaps*." She looked at him with concern as he started hyperventilating. "What's wrong with you?"

"Panic attack." He hunched over with his hands on his knees. "I wasn't expecting to be in here when this happened."

"We're trapped," Jenna said with mounting panic.

Dillon couldn't hide her contempt for her. "This isn't the time to panic. We're in here. We need to get out. So focus."

"How?" It took Kyle two breaths to say the single word.

"We have to figure a way to bring the rest of the shield down."

Jenna shook her head. "There must be rescue teams out there," she nodded beyond the shield. "We should find a place to lie low. Sit it out."

Dillon was about to scold her weakness – when fresh wails of terror flowed through the crowd. A massive wall of colorful balloons tied to a cart burst as a phantom soared through. It was the size of a sofa, sprinkling a constant stream of particles from its glistening, yellow skin. Three tentacles snaked around a vertical slash of a mouth large enough to swallow a man in half. It was almost comical.

Until it struck.

One little girl had been holding a red balloon she had plucked from the cart. She gazed directly up as the creature plummeted to the earth like a swooping eagle. The mouth opened three times as wide, forming a funnel that consumed the kid. When the phantom rose back into the air, there was no trace of the child save a puddle of ectoplasm. Even the balloon had gone.

The panicking crowd scattered in different directions, except for the shocked parents who hadn't seen the attack and were now searching around, shouting the child's name in vain. They didn't see a pair of sleek Class IV phantoms sweeping in.

Kyle couldn't take his eyes off them, as they were torn apart. Dillon tugged his arm.

"Let's go!"

"We have to help…" he said weakly.

"There's nothing we can do," she hissed. "Come on!"

She ran with the crowd. A glance behind showed Kyle and Jenna were following as the phantoms plowed through the fleeing guests.

Chapter 14

Terror Boulevard was one of the longest thoroughfares in the park, but it was twisted and subtly confused guest's inner geography, something that Wes was learning Elwood didn't possess. The design meant that key exhibits couldn't be seen from one area to the next. Even the Enclave, the largest structure in the park, remained out of sight until guests were in the aptly named Death Zone.

The ever-present light from the shield played over Tobias Elwood as he led the party straight down the center of the road. He gripped the vapo with both hands tightly so they couldn't see he was trembling. Sean walked alongside and hadn't stopped asking questions, not that Elwood had the opportunity or desire to answer them. The kid was constantly recollecting details from the Spook Hunters' show that Elwood had no memory of. Clarkson kept close behind, with the three dining staff between him and Lisa, who tightly clasped Emma's hand. Their heads never stopped darting nervously around.

Wes stayed several feet further back, armed with a vapo

he had retrieved from an emergency cache. A Tesla net was looped around his belt, next to a flashlight he'd taken from a dead security guard. He checked the radio. It was silent, jammed by the SkyShield.

Since leaving the diner, nobody had spoken a word to him. Elwood's public shaming had made him feel physically sick. Made worse by the fact it was all true. Inviting Lisa and the kids to the park tonight of all nights was proof positive that his life was just a string of wrong decisions.

Since scraping through college with a biology degree, nothing had gone the way he thought it would. Grand dreams involving world travel to exotic locations became unobtainable, while smaller ones – which were achievable by almost everybody else – were plucked just shy of victory. Every time he had picked himself up from defeat and marched on, confident that *next time* would be different. He had become convinced that it was always *somebody else* who had blocked his success; *somebody else* who failed to get back to him in time, or didn't do what was needed, or…

Now he realized it wasn't anybody else's fault. It was his own. The common denominator in all his failures was the guy looking at him in the mirror each morning. He thought his actions were well meaning, but Elwood and Clarkson had exposed him for the fraud he was. And Lisa had seen it too.

Any frail hopes he had of them getting together had been obliterated. Every step down the boulevard stirred the guilt plaguing him. He would do everything he could to get her and the kids out. Then he'd quit. Get in his car and drive off to some place else. Somewhere cold. Some place where dreams went to die.

He stopped walking and cocked his head.

"Hey!" he hissed. Only on the third attempt did Elwood stop and turn around.

"What is it, Talaska?" he said irritably.

Wes pointed to the sky. "Listen."

There was a collective holding of breath as everybody strained to hear whatever had alarmed him. A hundred foot above, the shield faintly hissed like a steak on a barbecue.

Elwood frowned. "It's the shield. So what?"

"What else can you hear?"

Elwood shook his head. "I can't hear anything. You must be imagining things."

"Exactly!" Wes waved his arms around, but nobody got it. He sighed. "The screaming. It's stopped."

Other than the background energy crackle, there was dead silence. Relieved smiles spread infectiously through the group.

"Well, that's a relief," Elwood said, lowering his weapon.

Clarkson lightly punched Elwood in the arm. "Way to go!"

Elwood un-modestly accepted the responsibility of bringing calm to the entire park. Becky gave a little sob of relief and hugged Scott, who was all too happy to hold her tight.

"Now let's get the hell out of here," Clarkson said, clapping his hands and rubbing them together.

Lisa's smile disappeared when she noticed the grave look on Wes' face.

"That's a good thing... isn't it?"

Wes looked nervously around. The weight of the gun was making his arm ache. "The shield's still up. The emergency bunkers were only designed to hold a hundred people at a time. There are five of them. What makes sixty thousand people suddenly fall silent?"

Nobody wanted to answer that, but the group drew closer together.

Elwood gestured to the darkness afforded by the trees on either side of the boulevard. "We should keep to the shadows."

"Why?" asked Sean. "They'll still be able to see us. They can see through a wider spectrum than–"

"Great, kid," snapped Elwood. Then he saw an abandoned tram further up the street. It had crashed into the front of a coffee store. The carriages were in a zigzag array behind. "Let's take the tram. It'll be quicker."

He walked towards it, but nobody else moved. Even from a dozen yards away they could see the seats were covered in dark stains. The tint from the SkyShield mercifully helped disguise the fact it was blood.

"I can walk faster than that," said Lisa.

"And it makes too much noise," added Wes, looking around.

Elwood huffed. "Then folks, we'll have to hot-foot it." The sweltering Nevada heat was already exhausting everybody. They weren't in a fit condition to run, no matter what was pursuing them. Elwood enthusiastically beckoned them onward.

"Not that way," Wes cautioned.

"That's the way to the hub, ain't it?" Elwood looked uncertain. "My sense of direction gets a little screwy in the dark."

"Sure. It goes straight there. And past just about every Class IV and V paddock we have." Wes took some delight in seeing Elwood's cocky grin vanish. "I think we should skirt around it." He pointed almost ninety degrees off-course.

"Are you kidding, Talasky?" growled Clarkson. "Even I

can see that's out of our way. Am I right?" He looked at Elwood, who gave an uncertain nod of confirmation. "Which is nothing but insanity."

"Maybe he has a point," said Lisa in a quiet voice.

Wes a surprised she was backing him up, but Clarkson quickly killed the moment.

"You're an employee, Lisa. At least for now. You don't have the benefit of an opinion."

Chagrinned, she looked away.

"Straight line, West," Elwood used a flat hand to gesture ahead. "Quickest route every time."

"Even if it passes the Enclave?"

Elwood paused mid-action. He had his back to the group, but Wes could sense his hesitation. He recovered quickly.

"But I think West here has read my mind," Elwood said without turning. "They'll be *expecting* us to go that way." He jinked his hand in the direction Wes indicated. "So if we curve around this way, we can stay stealthy." He turned to the group, his cocksure grin back in place. "Stay close to me and we'll make it."

"Good thinking," said Clarkson.

Wes couldn't figure out if the man was a complete moron, or in shock. He'd seen how fear could radically alter behavior. People would cling to the flimsiest of lies to convince themselves of a truth – from the fear of a failing relationship, the dread of facing financial hardships, or even ignoring a terrible illness, hoping it would go away. The primeval fear instinct promoted survival and kept people out of harm's way. But in the modern world it had become a pathological blindness that could lead to self-destruction as people ignored logic. The next fatal step was paralysis, liter-ally frozen to the spot.

And around the park's exhibits, that happened all too often.

Clarkson's sycophantic nodding galvanized the diner crew to follow Elwood as he broke into a light jog. Lisa kept her head bowed as she hurried to follow. Wes sighed. He swept his gaze behind them, searching for any sign they were being hunted. Then he followed. He gained a little satisfaction when he noticed the disappointment Sean was casting his TV hero.

The absence of screaming was more disturbing than the anguished cries. It was getting to Dillon, although she hid it from Kyle and Jenna. As a leader, she believed in portraying herself as an unshakable figure, no matter how much shit was striking the fan.

They had followed the crowd down a street that was covered by an ornate mesh canopy that would spray the crowds with a cooling mist. Without power, only the occasional warm drop of tepid water pattered down. Diners and stores had been abandoned, and some of the crowd broke away to take refuge in a large building with an entrance twisted into the shape of a maleficent clown's mouth. Designed to look like a nightmarish Gypsy carnival, Jenna had refused to follow them. Dillon was glad. She couldn't imagine why anybody would think it was a safe place to be.

"Sarah? Guys?"

Dillon was surprised to see Anna running towards them.

Spattered in dried blood that had matted her hair. It wasn't hers, although she looked like a survivor from a psychopath's rampage.

"Anna! Where are the others?"

Anna almost collapsed in Dillon's arms. Jenna spotted a vending machine that had toppled over, its soda cans strewn across the sidewalk. She took one, offering it to Anna. She opened the Pepsi with a shaking hand, gratefully gulping the liquid down her parched throat. She coughed and found her voice.

"Zane... he was... something got him. Tore him apart." She trembled uncontrollably.

"Easy, babe," said Kyle, rubbing her shoulders.

Then the sobbing started as Anna tried to speak.

Dillon backhanded her hard across the face. Anna reeled, dropping the Pepsi and regarding Dillon with contempt. There was blood on her lip, but whether it was hers, Dillon couldn't tell.

"Pull yourself together, Anna," Dillon growled. "We need you. You'll have plenty of time to breakdown when we get out of here. If you wanna cry now, you're dead already."

"Christ, Sarah, that's harsh..." Kyle began, but stopped when Anna blinked and nodded.

"Sorry... thanks." She closed her eyes and sucked in a long breath. "Zane's dead. All the charges went off early."

Kyle's brow furrowed. "He checked them. They were all fine."

"I saw some of them go off myself," Anna insisted, close to hysteria.

"Even if they were faulty, why would they go off at the same time?" said Dillon.

Anna shook her head. "They weren't faulty. I saw

Mike… he ran away from us. And then there was a detonation. He knew."

"Mike was with me," said Jenna. "In the Enclave. He left me. He ran out and left me."

Anna's eyes narrowed. "He was the one who caused this."

"Mike? Why would Mike do something like that?" Kylie said, looking nervously around as the last of the crowd dispersed.

Dillon knew the Welshman was fanatically opposed to the park, but setting the charges off early was detrimental to their cause. What had got into him?

Anna shivered. "Any word from Marv or Nathan? Any of the others?"

Dillon shook her head. "Nothing. The phones are down. You studied the electrical plans." Anna nodded. Dillon pointed to the SkyShield. "A substation must still be running. They mustn't have got there in time before all this went down."

Anna looked at her with wide eyes. "Are you nuts, Sarah? We can't stick to the plan. We have to get out of here." Her anxiety was rising.

Dillon struggled not to hit her again. "While that shield is up, we're not getting out. I need you to think, Anna. How to we shut it off? How do we get out of here?"

Anna saw the desperation in Jenna's and Kyle's eyes. There was none in Dillon's.

"There are two it could be…"

"Two?" Dillon bleated in despair.

Anna held up a finger as she tried to recall the plans. "One for the Enclave and one for that." She pointed upwards. If only she could remember which power station did which. Traveling to both would be impossible.

A chorus of wet shrieks rose from beyond the carnival entrance, causing all four of them to jump.

"Standing around here is going to get us killed," wheezed Kyle as he stepped back from the doorway.

Dillon nudged his arm. "Let's keep moving. Which way?" She looked at Anna hopefully.

Anna was on the verge of tears. She rubbed her face with both hands, inadvertently smearing the blood. "I need to think."

Dillon gently hooked Anna's arm and pulled her along until they were running.

"We'll figure it out on the way," she said gently, casting a look behind as terrible snarls issued from the doorway, silencing many of the screams. "But think, Anna. We're counting on you to get us out of here alive."

Chapter 15

The street ahead branched into narrow arteries representing Medieval European streets. The upper stories of the wattle and daub buildings curved inward and even touched at some points, giving the unsettling impression of walking through a ribcage. A dozen streets branched out, feeding into one another like a river delta.

"Apparition Alley," Sean breathed. He started to open his book. "It says here—"

Elwood irritably slammed the book shut. He squinted into the darkness.

"This is ambush central," he muttered.

Clarkson edged closer, making sure Elwood was between him and the potential horrors ahead.

"What are Apparitions?"

"They're bad," Elwood muttered.

Clarkson dropped to a whisper. "Everything here is bad."

Sean joined in with the whispering. "They suck the life

force out of your body and leave it as a dried up shell," he confided.

Clarkson shot Lisa a look. "You need to teach your kid to shut up."

Lisa's fists balled, but she said nothing. Wes took the lead, sniffing the air.

"This by-passes some of the nastier paddocks. I think we'll be okay."

"Based on what, Talasky?" Clarkson snapped.

"Based on the fact the shields that kept the Apparitions in here are all down and, as Sean could teach you, they're migrating creatures. They don't like being contained. Second, the only thing I can smell right now is your sweaty body odor. They smell like lavender."

Clarkson drew himself up to his full height, a good foot taller than Wes.

"You can't speak to me like that!"

"I don't work for you. I can speak to you any way I want, dickhead."

"I'm a paying guest!" he growled.

"I got you free tickets! Right now all you are to me is a decoy if things turn bad." Wes did not know where the jolt of courage came from. It made his head spin, but it was worth it to see the look on the bastard's face. He strode purposefully ahead. He resisted turning around, but the soft-shuffle of feet assured him the others were following. He was glad they couldn't see that he was shaking as he glanced fearfully from building to building. Elwood was right, it was ambush central.

The network of streets was cleverly designed to feel labyrinthine, but actually efficiently guided guests through at a steady rate to avoid any bottlenecks. A concealed sound system normally played ambient effects of life in the

Middle Ages, complete with subliminal cues to provoke a fear response. The confined route was so dark that Wes was forced to use his flashlight to highlight the way forward. He hated anything that would draw more attention to them. An extra beam from behind told him Elwood had done the same with the one built into the vapo.

They reached a small square where five passageways came together. In the center was a set of stocks on a raised dais. Around it lay three bodies, their skin parched and flaking. He cast his flashlight over them. Dried eyeballs had crumbled to dust. The skin had stretched and flaked so severely that lips were curled up in a death rictus. At first glance, they looked like poorly constructed prosthetic dummies, all part of the show, if it wasn't for their modern clothing.

He heard the gasps from behind as the others caught up, and he quickly moved the flashlight aside. A coffee store and a burger bar ruined the Medieval ambience. A yellow weapons cache was half concealed by the picnic tables bolted to the floor outside, but it was enough of a landmark for Wes to identify which passage to take onwards.

Sudden movement made Elwood around, and he fired a stream of Ion particles into the darkness. The coffee shop window exploded, and a bench was blasted in half before he heard the voices and released the trigger.

"STOP! STOP!" came a trembling voice from the dark. A portly Security Guard scrambled out with his hands raised. Shards of glass had drawn blood on his cheek and forehead. "Don't shoot!"

"Don't creep up on us like that!" Elwood snapped.

The guard looked at Elwood as if he was the Second Coming, despite being nearly killed by him. Tears rolled down his face. "Thank God it's you! Thank you! We've been hiding in there since the apparitions moved out."

"We?"

More movement from behind the guard had Elwood raising the vapo again as a large purple phantom loomed into view. Wes knocked the gun sideways. Elwood's shot took a chunk from the rooftop.

"Whoa! Captain Trigger Happy, stop shooting!" Wes hissed. "You're drawing attention to us!"

Elwood pointed at the phantom, but said nothing when he realized it was Phamo, the park mascot. The oversized cartoon suit was dirty and singed. Half his head had been blown away from the first attack. The actor yanked the head off, revealing Stuart inside.

"You almost killed me!" he howled.

"What do you expect, walking around dressed like that?" Elwood protested.

"All I've got a pair of boxers on under this, and nothing else!" Stuart snapped. His anger subsided a little when he saw Wes. "Is it over? Are they contained?"

Wes shook his head. "Everything's down. It's catastrophic."

"I knew it." The guard looked at Stuart, picking up an earlier conversation. "I told you what I saw, and you didn't believe me."

"What did you see?" Wes prompted.

The guard rubbed a bump on his head. "A couple of bozos attacked me near the C-block substation." He waved in the vague direction. "They were dressed like a maintenance crew, but looked real shifty. When I asked for ID, they whacked me on the head. Knocked me out." He frowned as he tried to recall. "When I came too, smoke was pouring from the substation. Something had exploded inside. People were screaming as all heck broke loose."

"Terrorists," growled Elwood. "What kind of sicko–"

"Can you smell that?" said Scott suddenly. When Phamo had appeared, he'd been the first to retreat back the way they came. "Smells like flowers."

Wes sniffed the air, following the scent – straight to the teenager. "Run!"

Scott did – unfortunately in the wrong direction.

He sprinted straight into the arms of an Apparition as it phased from a wall. It was an eight-foot humanoid, stick thin and with pale, luminous flesh. Slender hands gripped the side of the teen's head and its mouth opened wide. The kid couldn't utter any noise louder than a gargle as every molecule of moisture was sucked from his body, through his head. He violently spasmed as bones cracked and skin turned as dry as parchment. The Apparition's gangly body swelled. Popping and expanding as it inhaled the human.

Elwood roared with fury and unleashed his vapo.

"NO!" Wes' warning came too late.

The Ion stream burned through Scott's diner uniform and blasted his desiccated corpse into a cloud of ash, before passing through the Apparition and puncturing a hole through more tables, blasting apart the weapons cache and the fiberglass wall behind.

Wes blindly grabbed the person nearest to him, Ralph, and shoved him towards a branching passageway. "That way! Run!"

The others followed. Sensing its prey was escaping, the apparition lumbered forward. Its long legs slowly propelling it as if it was running on the moon. Elwood fired again – just as Clarkson cut across his path. The edge of the stream struck his thigh and sent Clarkson tumbling into the bodies around the stock. His weight crushed the fragile corpses to dust. The apparition deviated course for the stricken member of the herd.

"Vapos don't work on them!" said Wes.

Elwood let the weapon drop on its strap around his shoulder. "How should I know? I never hunted these things!"

Before he could respond, Wes saw Sean running towards the broken weapons cache. "Sean!" Lisa and Emma were already at the entrance of the far passage before she noticed. Wes sprinted across to him. "What are you doing?" he stopped when Sean triumphantly raised a small pistol from the items that had fallen from the broken weapons cache.

Wes couldn't help but smile. "You genius!"

He snatched the taser. Turned, and fired, as the Apparition loomed over Clarkson. An array of metal darts thudded into the back of the creature and instantly sent a powerful electrical wave through it. It let out a high-pitch squeal as it tumbled to the floor, writhing in agony.

Sean punched the air victoriously. "We're hunters now!"

Elwood and Phamo lifted Clarkson, slinging his arms over their shoulders, and rushed to join the others in the passage. Wes took Sean's hand, and they brought up the rear, giving the thrashing Apparition a wide berth.

Nobody said a word until the arcing passage widened, depositing them on another wide avenue lined with benches and far enough from any buildings so they could see danger arrive. Clarkson was dropped onto a bench. He twisted his leg to see the wound. Beneath a smoldering hole in his suit trousers, the flesh was red and bloody.

"I can't feel my leg!" he whimpered. "Who knows first aid?" He stared at Lisa. She shook her head.

"You wouldn't let me take the course." She folded her arms.

"You'll live," said Elwood. "I've had a few similar scrapes in the past." He looked curiously at Sean, who was enduring another long hug from his mother. "Hey kiddo, how did you know about using the taser?"

Sean frowned and held up the encyclopedia he still clung to. "It's in *your* book."

"Quick thinking, Tobias," said Clarkson. Ralph and the Security Guard nodded in agreement.

Wes lost his shit. "Are you kidding? *Captain Semper Fi* here has never *read* that thing!" He caught Sean's confusion. "It's ghost written."

Sean and Emma exchanged an impressed look.

"Wow! You got a ghost to write it?" Emma said.

Wes sighed. "No. I mean…" he gave up and turned to survey the route ahead. A river ran parallel to the avenue. Upstream, a broad stone bridge adorned with gruesome gargoyles crossed it, leading to another section. "We're not too far from the hub. It's just on the other side of that."

A sign in a curling gothic script read: SPECTER-VILLE.

Chapter 16

"This is a bad idea," Lisa said, drawing Sean and Emma closer as they stepped onto the bridge. Once over the river they would enter the dubiously named Specter-Ville.

Wes tried to reassure her. "Don't let the name put you off. This is like Main Street. The Specter Corrals are way over there. The river loops around it, and a lot of phantoms don't like water. It's one of the safest areas we can be." He could see that she wasn't convinced. "Out the other side and it's a hundred-yard dash to the command hub."

"Then we'll be safe?" Emma asked in a small voice.

As safe as running through the Masai Mara daubed in blood, Wes thought gloomily. The fear generated by thousands of guests trapped in an enclosed space would've created a feeding frenzy for the park's denizens. Who knew what it would take to stop that cycle?

He looked at the faces of the others. Clarkson was strung between Phamo and Ralph, his face scrunched in pain every time he put weight on his injured leg. The others looked desperate and frightened. Becky hadn't stopped sobbing since the death of her colleague, a man who Wes suspected had been her boyfriend.

Wes's dreams were shattered, but hers had been torn asunder in an act of violence by a wild animal. Wes was having difficulty blaming the creatures themselves. They were feral, forcibly relocated for entertainment by people who didn't really understand what they were dealing with. His eyes fell on Elwood, who stood a little way ahead, acting as the hero, but his swagger was missing without his support team and the cameras. Wes was now regarding him as the poster boy for everything that was wrong with this place.

"Wes?" Lisa's eyes searched his. She needed hope, not the truth.

"Completely safe," he assured her. And in doing so, felt more wretched than he had all day.

The group entered the wide oval plaza. Dozens of eateries and stores lined the periphery. Meals lay discarded on the tables of the large outdoor dining area. The shops were crammed with merchandise, most of which was now cast in the streets, since windows had been broken and the interiors ransacked. T-shirts, replica weapons, and action figures were strewn everywhere. Elwood kicked a plush phantom that was covered in ectoplasm and torn in half by razor-sharp teeth.

Other avenues met here from every compass point. Five massive fountains depicting various pan-creatures usually played a coordinated light and water show every fifteen minutes. Now they lay dark, silent and sinister.

The centerpiece of the plaza was a three-story Museum of the Supernatural, its curved architecture inspired by Gaudi. The stained-glass windows were smashed, and thick orange flames curled from within. The intense heat from the inferno could be felt hundreds of yards away. The fire cast flickering shadows over the bodies strewn around the plaza.

"What got them?" Stuart struggled to keep the emotion from his voice.

Elwood and Wes swapped a look before slowly approaching the nearest body. It was a park technician. Thankfully, she lay face down, but a huge chunk had been taken from her back, ripping a gaping hole in her uniform through which internal organs could be seen. Her right arm had been severed.

Wes struggled not the throw up. Elwood winced, but was keeping it together surprisingly well.

"I've seen wounds like this before," he breathed. "Russia. Out on the Steppe..."

"Specters!" Sean spoke up, standing on tiptoes to see what they were looking at. Wes sidestepped to block his view. "You hunted down specters in Russia!"

Elwood nodded solemnly. "They're the worst kinds. The Scandis are nasty. The Africans, they're killers. The Russian specters. They're smart." That trip had been a disaster. Two of the crew had died, which had given Spook Hunters the unsettling reputation for being the deadliest television show to work on.

"The Corral must've gone down," Elwood said as quietly as he could.

Wes slung the vapo over his shoulder, then slid the Tesla net from his belt. The tungsten net had a thumb-sized controller. A wheel that allowed the charge to be raised or lowered, with a small set of LEDs indicating the intensity. Weighted edges allowed it, if thrown correctly, to soar through the air like a bolas. Once it wrapped around a target, it would discharge its powerful force.

Elwood spotted another Tesla net discarded on the floor. He shouldered his rifle and took it.

"No point in loitering," he said to the others, flashing his trademarked smile. "Stick close."

They made their way across the plaza, slowed down by a limping and grumbling Clarkson. They reached the north plaza entrance and Wes realized his mistake. The path was blocked by a large gate that kept the public from seeing the more utilitarian maintenance roads. It was only opened for emergencies and parade vehicles.

He ran his fingers across the dark card scanner on the wall. Without power, the hydraulic gate wouldn't easily open. Wes dug his fingers in the narrow gap at the edge of the gate, placed a foot against the wall, and heaved with all his weight. It didn't budge.

Wes grunted as he tried again. "Give me a hand." He grew impatient when Elwood didn't respond. "I can't do this on my..."

He trailed off when he noticed Elwood was walking away from him. Everybody had turned to watch three specters emerge from the burning museum. The flames licked their skin, but didn't harm them. They were huge. Some twelve feet long and five across the shoulders. Serpent-like heads drifted side-to-side as they searched for the scent of their victims. The scent of fear.

Then they slowly, inexorably, turned towards the group trapped in the northern section of the plaza.

"Get that door open, West," Elwood said, activating the Tesla net with his thumb. The control lit up in his hand. At that same moment, the alpha specter swooped directly for them, while the other two cut across the plaza, following the curve of the far buildings in order to zero in on them from the opposite direction.

"Help me with the gate!" Wes said as he tried to heave it open again.

Ralph and Lisa joined him, pushing it with everything they had. The gate's wheels squealed as they fractionally moved. Elwood swung the net in his right hand, the weighted edges expanding out. He took several steps towards the alpha that was hurtling towards him.

"It's moving…" gasped Wes.

"Hurry!" Elwood urged. He flung the Tesla net at the creature. He had been instrumental in refining their usage and design. He was also a crack shot. The net expanded right into the path of the specter and folded around its body. Elwood waited for the deafening crack as it discharged.

Instead, there came a tinny crackling noise, and a synthesized electronic scream.

"GOT ONE!" declared a poor recording of Elwood.

"It's a freakin' toy!" wailed Elwood.

It had been realistic enough to make the alpha deviate from its path and caused the other two killers to hesitate. The plastic net was torn apart by the specter.

Stuart yelled in terror and ran for another road leading out of the plaza.

Wes stopped heaving at the gate and tried to follow him. "Stuart! No!"

Elwood's powerful arms yanked Wes to a halt. Running from a specter was an open invitation to be pursued. The alpha flew in a tight spiral as it vectored in on him. Dressed in the cumbersome purple Phamo suit, Stuart made a pitiful figure as the predator cannoned into him. Stuart's screams changed pitch as he was thrust to the floor. Powerful jaws bit into him. The other two specters veered towards the blood, trying to snatch a limb for themselves.

Wes choked back a sob as he saw a cartoon leg torn free

and tossed into the air – where it was plucked by a scavenging beast. As two specters tore into the body, the third looked sharply up, reveling in the human's fear response. With a cackle, it flew straight for them.

Elwood went for his gun. "Oh, crap…"

"Get the gate," Wes said as he unfurled his Tesla net.

Elwood didn't argue. Wes swung the net over his head, just as he'd been shown in training. He tried to ignore that this was his first live trial. And if he got it wrong, it would be his last.

The specter's streamlined head put him in mind of a shark as it sliced through the air. Wes didn't dare blink as he released the net. It blossomed open – and the creature flew straight into it. The weighted edges snapped around it, and the electric discharge sounded like a clap of thunder. The creature issued a pathetic squeal as it dropped from the air and bounced from the ground twice before sliding to a stop at Wes's feet. It shuddered, ectoplasm oozing from it. It wasn't dead, just solidified. Which meant it was vulnerable.

Wes fired his vapo point blank. The supercharged ion stream blew the head off the specter. Ectoplasm and bile sprayed everywhere. Unlike the phantoms, this creature wouldn't start reforming. It was dead.

"Come on!" Elwood yelled as he shouldered the gate aside just enough for everyone to slip through. Wes gave one last sad look at Stuart's body before running to join them. He saw Elwood's eyes widen as he looked beyond Wes.

"Faster, West. *Much* faster!"

Wes didn't need to look behind to see the danger. He powered forward – throwing himself headlong through the narrow gap. Now on the other side of the door, Elwood began heaving the gate closed.

"What are you doing?" Wes exclaimed. "They can phase right through it!"

Elwood wasn't thinking. He stopped pushing and ran. Through the gap, they could see the remaining two specters cautiously flying towards them.

The service road leading into the plaza crossed over a small humpback bridge. On the river below, three small boats, designed to look like ghostly galleons, slowly drifted past on the current. The Rabid Rapids ride was a leisurely loop around the park. With the pumps off, the current was sluggish, but with several hundred thousand tons of water in the system, the lack of power would not stop the boats moving any time soon. Beyond, the road led a hundred yards to the dark command bunker and the wide service area behind.

"There it is!" yelled Wes, feeling a second wind. "Go! Go!"

Everybody ran to the bridge.

With a dull plop, the specters phased through the gate, leaving a smattering of ectoplasm in their wake. They sharply veered aside to avoid crossing the water, a maneuver that allowed Lisa and the kids to reach the bridge. Ralph and the Security Guard had Clarkson between them, blocking the way.

"Move it!" Lisa snapped.

With a shriek, the alpha specter surged across the bridge, which saved it from any contact with the water. Everybody hit the deck – except the guard. He was hauled off his feet and lifted, kicking and screaming, fifteen feet into the air.

Lisa was pinned by Clarkson and Becky. She looked frantically around.

"Sean? Emma?"

"We're okay!" replied Sean.

"Help me up!" pleaded Clarkson as the second specter advanced towards them.

Lisa and Becky stood, stringing her boss between them.

"Run! Don't stop! Don't look behind. Just run!" yelled Wes – just as Elwood fired at the charging specter.

The Ion stream hit it head on. Although it didn't cause any physical damage, the creature dropped from the air and thudded to the ground. It snarled with rage, pulling itself towards the humans using its two long arms.

"GO! GO!" Elwood yelled as he and Wes provided covering fire.

Lisa clenched her teeth as she bore Clarkson's weight. The entrance to the bunker was tantalizingly within reach. Dim emergency lights illuminated the front. There was an awful scream from behind as the alpha hurled the Guard into the concrete floor. She could hear bones snap from the impact, but didn't look back.

Wes overtook her and slapped his access card against the door scanner. The heavy door slid open, and Lisa and Becky blundered inside, unceremoniously dropping a complaining Clarkson to the floor.

Lisa heard raised voices of concern as the bunker staff ran to help them, but her legs gave way and she slid to the ground, sobbing with relief. With a crump, the bunker door closed. Everybody stopped to catch their breaths. They were safe.

Elwood pressed the barrel of his vapo against the door's lock and squeezed the trigger. Smoke poured from the lock as the plastic and electronics bubbled.

Lisa looked around. "Emma?" cold fear gripped her heart. She stood, frantically searching the dimly lit control room. "Where's Sean? Where are my kids?" She looked accusingly at Elwood, who had been the one to seal them inside.

"I thought they were with you!" he said.

"They must be still outside…" Wes said with a knot in his throat.

Then the pounding began as the two specters attempted to breach the security door.

Chapter 17

"Open it up right now!" Lisa screamed as she lunged for Elwood. She landed a punch in his chest before Blake hooked an arm around her waist and pulled her back. She lashed out with both legs, landing a pair of satisfying kicks.

"I didn't know!" wailed Elwood.

Lisa shrugged Blake off. "Open the door!"

"Whoa! Easy! We can't. Elwood blew the lock."

"My children are out there!"

"I need a God-damned medic!" Clarkson howled. Lisa reeled on him – but lapsed into silence as the pounding from outside abruptly stopped. Everybody strained to listen.

Clarkson fearfully eyed the door. "Where'd they go?"

"Russian specters are smart," Blake said confidently. "They know they can't get through a shielded door."

"My kids..." Lisa broke into tears.

"What kind of mother are you? Bringing your kids to a damned theme park," Clarkson muttered in pain. Ying crouched next to him and jabbed an anesthetic into his thigh, before using scissors to cut the rest of his expensive suit trousers off so she could treat the wound.

Wes watched Lisa slide down the wall. She hugged her knees and cried. He resisted the urge to comfort her. Instead, he hurried across to Tanaka. "Get the cameras up."

"They've been down since the outage. We've barely got enough power to run this joint, keep the shield up, and the big guy in."

All eyes went to the map on the screen, and the reassuring pulse of light still around the Enclave.

"Is anybody coming to help us out?" Wes glanced between the technicians, who all avoided looking at him.

Blake heaved a long sigh and slumped into his chair. "We've no contact with the outside world. The shield acts as one big radio jammer. If we go by the playbook, then there is a small ancillary team based at McCarran who should be trying to reinstate power. The thing is, they should have done that in the first thirty minutes. We don't know what's working or not working."

"Terrorists," said Elwood. His voice lacked his usual arrogance, as he kept flicking sidelong glances at Lisa. Wes had seen the repercussions of fear. It bore the hallmarks of post-traumatic stress disorder, and Tobias Elwood was suffering from it. "We met a security guard who was attacked by a bunch of them at a substation. This was a deliberate act of sabotage."

Everybody began talking at once. Wes was vaguely aware of the names and theories being tossed around. His attention was on the map, and the Rabid Rapid river snaking through the park. It cut from one side to the other, through some of the most dangerous paddocks.

Ignoring the heated discussion, Wes crossed to Tanaka at his desk.

"Are you able to power the cameras if you divert power from here?"

"You mean from our life support systems? Sure, but… that would mean compromising the bunker's own shielding." They both knew the only thing that had kept the specters out had been the Tesla charge radiating through the walls.

"The cameras don't use that much juice."

"Sure, even so, if the integrity drops, they could get in."

Wes leaned closer and lowered his voice. "We just need it for a few minutes. Those specters won't be hanging outside. They've got the attention spans of a teenager. They're gone already. I just need the cameras on the Rapids."

Tanaka followed his gaze to Lisa, who was leaning against the wall, head in her hands and ignoring the heated conversation as Blake squeezed every bit of information from the survivors. He sighed and accessed the power management software. His fingers rattled across the keys.

"Why the river?"

"Because Sean's a smart kid. He knows more than most the people working in this park."

"Spooks don't like water…"

"Exactly. Most of them anyway," he amended. "And if they were outside when the doors shut…" He couldn't reach the gruesome conclusion.

"We'd have heard the screams," said Tanaka.

Wes nodded.

"Okay. Here we go." There was the faintest flicker from the lighting system as power diverted. Wes heard the air conditioning whine down, but only because he was listening for it. "I can't get them all up in one go. I'll have to cycle through the sectors. Let's start with where you lost them."

The security cameras outside the Specter-Ville north gate came online. The river curved around the back of the plaza buildings and under the bridge they had escaped over. A couple of the galleon rides bobbed along at a walking pace, borne by the current. The dissected remains of the security guard could clearly be seen. There was no sign of the specters or the children.

"Follow the current." Wes walked closer to the wall screen, scanning each of the images as they cycled through the cameras along the bank. He knew vaguely that the discussion in the room had stopped.

"Are the shields down?" Blake asked nervously. Tanaka nodded, but Blake held back his anger as he picked up on Wes's plan.

The cameras took several seconds to power up between each section. The river meandered through dark forests and haunted bayous, each showing empty miniature galleons. Occasionally, the odd body could be seen on the riverbanks, but Wes tried not to dwell on them.

Lisa joined him. "Why are you looking at the river?"

"They were on the bridge. If they'd jumped down on the boats, it would have been the safest place to be."

"Emma can't swim."

Wes said nothing. The camera was about to cycle to the next batch when Wes raised his hand.

"Hold it!" He edged closer to the screen, peering at a lone galleon. Then he saw movement. Even with the high-definition night vision cameras, it almost went unseen – but it was definitely the head of a child poking from just above the gunwale. In proportion to the tiny ghost ship, it looked as if a giant was onboard. There was no mistaking Sean.

Lisa sobbed with relief, clasping her hands over her mouth.

Wes hurried to the desk where he had laid his vapo. "The moment I'm through the door, put the shields back up."

Blake shook his head. "You can't go outside, Wes. *Everything* is out there."

"It's my fault they're here. I'm going to get them."

"And the door lock is still jammed. They're safe on the boat and are a quarter of the way around the park already. Most things out there avoid water. You'll get yourself killed for nothing. If they stay put, they'll float right past the door again and we can get them then."

Wes hesitated. He looked at the map. "Where are they?"

Tanaka checked his screen. "Camera B2014... Oh..."

"What?"

"They're about to enter the *Umibozu Numachi*."

Wes dropped the vapo back down on the table with a loud thud.

"Shit."

Lisa looked at him in alarm. "*Umibozu Numachi?* What's that?"

The boat shimmied as it took another bend in the river. The ten-foot-long ghost ship's fiberglass hull was contained by submerged rails to keep the rides in the center of the channel. The operational noises were usually concealed by ghostly sound effects piped from hidden speakers, but with no power, every mechanical squeal was amplified in the darkness.

The bench seats carried twelve guests at a time, but Sean and Emma were the only ones onboard, hunkered in the rear footwell and protected from behind by a mock-fore-castle that curved partially above them.

When the specters had attacked the bridge, Sean had taken his sister's hand, and they had jumped over the parapet onto the passing boat. Scared of drawing attention to themselves, they'd hidden between the seats, only emerging when the boat had taken them a safe distance away.

"How do we get off?" Emma whispered as she gazed at the far bank. The water seemed alive as it reflected the crackling SkyShield. It was like being sandwiched in a kalci-doscope.

"We can swim for it."

"I can't swim. And you know that."

Their mother had never taken them swimming, claiming that she never had the time. Her usual excuse. Sean had been dozens of times with his friend's parents. They had taught him to swim. Living in the middle of a desert, it had felt like a luxury.

"I bet it's not deep." Sean peeked over the edge. It was impossible to judge. He had often looked at maps of the park, tracing his finger along the Rapid Rapids and imag-ined what wonders they would see. Now he was here, he was slightly disappointed to be staring at empty paddocks as they passed. He recalled the map.

"We're close to the landing stage where you're supposed to get on." He had seen it dozens of times on TV. Watching wide-eyed and soaked guests debarking and grinning with insane delight. Without power, he knew the ride would just be dull, with none of the hidden jets of water and artificial whirlpools. He was surprised to realize that calm was what he wanted right now. His sister usually cried over the slightest thing at home, which he suspected was calculated to get him into trouble. Yet out here, as the park fell apart around them, she was silent and alert. She was also frightened out of her mind. "We can jump off there. And you won't get wet."

"Promise?"

"Promise. Anyway, we're safe here. Phantoms don't like water."

"Why not?"

He shrugged. "Something to do with it breaking down the ectoplasm."

She smiled, more afraid of the water than the phantoms. They lapsed into silence for a few minutes. Sean trailed his hand over the edge, cutting it through the water. He occasionally splashed a palmful across his face to cool him down. It was much hotter than it should be at this time of night.

"I wish dad was here," he blurted. He didn't know where that had come from. In fact, he could barely remember his dad, but in his mind, he associated him as a more capable parent than their mom. He knew that wasn't fair. Their mom was always there, but other than running them to and from school and preparing meals, there was little other social activity. She was either working on the phone or looking sad.

"I don't remember him," Emma whispered. "He never came to see me."

She had spoken to him a few times over Skype, but she was two when he last came to visit. And that was a lifetime ago.

"Do you think he'll ever come back?"

Sean shook his head. He'd long ago stopped hoping for such a thing.

Emma suddenly shook his arm and pointed ahead. "Look at that!"

The surrounding landscape was changing, becoming more swamp-like, with trees crowning the bank and casting long trailing branches into the water. The air was alive with the sound of frogs, adding to the swamp ambience. Sticking out of the water was a thirty-foot tall Japanese Torii gate. It looked ancient and decrepit. They passed silently underneath, noticing the claw marks in the wood around the supporting legs.

Sean gasped. *"Umibozu Numachi!"* the name was emblazoned over his map at home and in his encyclopedia, and he had been proud when he was able to pronounce the unfamiliar name. He'd even learned a few other Japanese phrases for good measure. As usual, his mother hadn't been impressed. She hadn't really listened. She never did.

"What does that mean?"

"Numachi is Japanese for 'swamp'. The *Umibozu* are water spirits." He clutched his book, which was still with him, despite all the odds. It was too dark to read, but it felt like a comfort blanket.

They hunkered low, peering over the benches as the boat turned another tight bend, revealing a Japanese village on the bank. The Edo-period buildings appeared long-abandoned and were artfully covered in vines and moss. Another torii was angled, poised to crash into the water – which it would have done if the hydraulic system was operational.

Their attention was suddenly drawn to a small, dark

figure at the foot of the gate as it slipped into the water with a barely perceptible plop.

Emma stiffened. "I thought you said ghosts don't like water."

"There are some exceptions," he whispered back.

They scanned the water's surface for any betrayal of movement.

"What do they look like?" Emma whispered.

"There are only drawings of them in my book. They can't be photographed."

"And what do they do to people?"

"They eat them."

They both flinched as five slender fingers, each six-inches long and tipped with black nails, gripped the edge of the prow. The Umibozu pulled itself from the water, silhouetted against the glowing sky. A pair of webbed feet gripped the gunwale, and the creature squatted. Its round head jerked like a bird's as it sniffed for any signs of life. It was no bigger than Sean, but it oozed menace.

Then it opened its eyes.

They glowed bright white. Almost perfect circles like car headlights. The mist rising from the water highlighted the beams as they came to rest on the first bench. The Umibozu crept forward on all-fours, sniffing the air and scanning its beams side-to-side. Able to only see what was illuminated in those short pools of light, it relied on an acute sense of smell, from which it could build a detailed map of its environment. Water vapor rose from its body as it slunk across to the second bench, peering in the footwells between the seats.

Emma held her breath to stop screaming. Sean was transfixed by the creature. Now it was closer, he could just make out a thin mouth and matted silver hair across its body. With every breath Sean took, he could taste and smell the rank odor of rotting fish emanating from it.

He nudged Emma and slid a taser from his belt. He'd had taken the second weapon from Apparition Alley, and had kept it concealed under his shirt, knowing his mother would have confiscated it the moment she saw it. Now it was about to save their lives.

The Umibozu stretch across onto the third bench. The leading beams of light sliding from the seat and into the last footwell where the children were. Sean was almost blinded as the lights zeroed in on him.

The creature gave a shrill howl of surprise that sent goosebumps racing over the children's skin. Sean raised the taser between the blazing eyes and he fired.

The flechettes buried into thc Umibozu's skull and unleashed their powerful charge. The creature reeled back-wards in pain, slipping from the side of the boat, clutching its face. It was dead before it hit the water.

"That was awesome!" Emma shrieked.

Sean's hand was trembling as he kept the taser level. "I saw Elwood do something similar in season two."

He saw the gun was covered in ectoplasm, as was his hand and sleeve. It hissed and stung his skin.

"That looks like snot!" said Emma.

Sean lay the taser on a bench and leaned over the side to wash the gunk off. The cool water numbed the pain. At the last moment, he saw two glowing orbs in the water below. He gasped in fright and pulled himself back into the boat as a second Umibozu shot from the water and over his head. It landed in the middle of the boat with enough force to precariously rock it. Emma was pitched towards the edge with a yelp.

Then she toppled into the river.

Sean reached out for her – but pulled his hand back as the Umibozu's talon slashed at him. The mesmerizing glowing eyes fixed on him. He raised one arm to shield his eyes–

While the other groped for the taser.

It wasn't there. The sudden movement had knocked it into a dark footwell. His probing hand touched the encyclopedia. Using all his strength, Sean swung the heavy book and cracked it across the Umibozu's skull.

The creature shrieked and slipped off the bench and into a footwell. Sean threw the book as hard as he could at the glowing eyes. He heard a crunch and another gibber of pain. Then he jumped over the side.

The SkyShield offered just enough light for him to see Emma struggling in the water. Her head kept dipping under the surface, silencing any calls for help as she drowned. He powered towards her, his arms aching from the effort.

"I've got you!" He hooked an arm under her chin, forcing her head just above the water. She thrashed in panic, her arm smacking across his face and threatening to push him under the surface. "Stop struggling or you'll drown us both!"

His words got through, and Emma stopped thrashing. Kicking in a backstroke, Sean reached the bank. They were both relieved to feel slick mud ooze between their fingers as they dragged themselves out of the river.

Their boat was already vanishing around another bend downstream. Any hopes that the Umibozu was still onboard were dashed when they saw movement in the water. A round head broke the surface, and a pair of glowing eyes circled around, searching for them.

Sean nudged Emma and indicated to the top of the bank. "We're too far for it to see us. Let's go!"

As silently as they could, they scrambled up the mud on all-fours.

Utter silence gripped the command hub as everybody watched the children's plight unfold on the screen. Even if Wes had commandeered a gas-powered jeep, he was still too far away to have made it in time.

A cheer erupted when a camera picked up Sean and Emma clambering over the lower wall of a powered-down Tesla shield as they left the Japanese village behind and ran across a road.

"We can't just sit here!" snapped Wes. He had hoped they'd stayed on the relative safety of the boat, but now, out in the open, they were easy pickings. He snatched his vapo from the desk again.

"Wes, they could run anywhere. The radios are down. There's no way we could tell you where they've gone."

"I'll take my chances."

"Wait!" said Elwood, pointing to a screen. "There they are. Camera G7652."

The children were running towards a partially open metal door. It obviously wasn't part of an exhibit. It was a functional maintenance entrance.

"Smart kids!" said Sophie, with a relieved chuckle. "Keep away from the enclosures."

Lisa was bewildered. She had watched events unfold in

mute silence, unable to tear her gaze away. She felt like the worst mother in the world, and helpless with it.

"Find out which block that is."

"Uh, Wes…" Tanaka looked pale.

Everybody followed his gaze to the camera feed on-screen. They watched as the children pulled the door wider and slipped inside.

"Do we have cameras inside?" said Wes.

Tanaka shook his head and zoomed the image further out.

They watched as the outbuilding door shrank away, revealing the complex beyond. The only sound in the room was a cry of despair from Lisa.

Chapter 18

The dark service corridor was so humid that a thin mist hung in the air. Sean knew he was gripping Emma's hand too tightly, but she didn't complain. A purple pulsing light at the end of the passage beckoned them forward.

"I'm scared," Emma whispered.

"You're supposed to be." Sean wasn't sure where his bravado was coming from. Thinking about their parents had angered him, and perhaps that was just enough to override the terror he should be feeling. "The park has lots of roads and equipment stores underground, away from the guests. I read about them on the internet. There are these big panic rooms where hundreds of people can hide if there's an emergency."

"Is this one of them?"

"I hope so."

Sean didn't quite believe it. The complete lack of signs worried him. A glass box on the wall caught his attention. A fire extinguisher was hooked outside, while behind the glass was a fire ax.

"Stand back." He removed the extinguisher and took several steps back, before hurling it at the glass. The shattering was overly loud and caused Emma to jump.

"Can you do that?" she asked, open-mouthed.

"I'm twelve. I can do anything." Sean carefully lifted the ax down. The wooden handle was warm to the touch, and it weighed more than he expected. Hefting it with both hands, he nodded onwards. "Let's go."

Crackling sounded beyond the partially open far door. Sean used the heavy iron ax head to nudge it wider. They entered a large circular chamber. The far screen ahead glowed with bright purple Tesla energy so that everything between them and it was in silhouette. They glimpsed a large figure looming over them, before a flash from the screen illuminated a terrifying canine-headed figure.

Emma screamed.

Sean swung the ax with a yell. The blade arced and thudded into their attacker, making an unusual hollow sound as it bit into a muscular human leg. The impact jarred the ax out of his hand, and it remained in the leg. It wasn't until a series of flashes from the screen beyond illuminated the fiberglass statue that Sean had assaulted.

It was a realistic depiction of the ancient Egyptian God, Anubis. its fierce jackal head was set in a wide snarl. Behind them, more were more towering statues depicting the multi guises of the Angel of Death. They were all poised over a tram approach road.

Sean slowly turned to the pulsing shield. A huge dark shadow restlessly soared back and forth, aggravating the screen. Emma's shriek had alerted it to the children's presence. He snatched Emma's arm, but she was frozen in place. She knew exactly where they were.

Static hissed in their ears, playing a variety of different

languages, until locking onto English. It was a pleading, sibilant voice, low and seductive.

"*Reeeleassee meee….*"

"How's that lock coming?" Wes demanded.

Hugh jammed a screwdriver into the door's locking panel and jiggled the metal cover plate away. It clanged to the floor, revealing the physical locking mechanism.

"Almost there."

Wes adjusted the strap of the vaporizer around his neck. The moment he had seen the children enter the Enclave; he knew something had to be done.

"I'm coming with you," said Lisa firmly, securing her hair in a tight ponytail.

"It's not safe."

"They're my children." She tilted her head defiantly. Wes looked away, unable and unwilling to argue.

"Elwood, are you ready?" The telling silence from behind made him slowly turn.

Tobias Elwood was still staring at the blank screens, clutching his vapo in one hand. Tanaka had been forced to cut the cameras and divert the power back to the bunker's systems. Without air con, it was already cloyingly warm, and any condensation risked damaging the delicate computer systems. There was also the unspoken fact that everybody wanted the room shielded once again.

"Elwood?" Wes prompted.

Elwood slowly turned and noticed everybody was looking at him expectantly.

"If the kids stay there, they'll be safe."

"What?"

"Think about it. It's the safest place in the park. All the other spooks are giving the Enclave a wide berth. Even they're terrified of what's in there…" He immediately regretted saying that.

"That's exactly why we need to get them out!"

Clarkson spoke up. The anesthetic had sedated him for a short while, but since Ying had treated his wound, but his arrogance was returning.

"If he goes with you, who's going to protect us?"

Wes was incredulous. "They're kids!"

"And this place is all that's stopping the hordes of hell from getting out!" Clarkson snapped.

Elwood couldn't look at Wes.

"Elwood, come on. This place is shielded…"

Elwood nodded at Clarkson. "He's right. Somebody needs to stay here and watch over them. This place is vital. I'll do it." He had the audacity to sound reluctant.

Lisa approached him, laying a hand on his trunk-like biceps. "Tobias, I need your help. They're my children. They worship you. You're the action guy. You're their hero."

"I'm sorry, sweetheart. I'm needed here. West'll do just fine." Aghast, Lisa snatched her hand away. Elwood searched for something to say. "The needs of the many outweigh the needs of–"

"Cut the bullshit!" Wes barked. "What happened to 'Time to Fry' and all that crap? I can't do this on my own!" Elwood's gaze bore into the floor, his conscience nagging him. "I thought you thrived on this? Three seasons and God knows how many awards?"

Lisa reacted when she saw Elwood brush a tear aside.

"I'm not... I can't..." he was suddenly hyperventilating. "All that stuff... Afghanistan... the Marine core. I was the only survivor because I ran away!" His confession echoed around the stunned room.

Blake was the first to find his voice. "You tell us this now?"

Elwood slumped on the edge of a desk and exhaled as he relived the moment. "When that first shot rang out... I got scared. I turned tail. Left my squad behind..." He put his head in his hands and sobbed. "When they found out, I was dishonorably discharged."

Another round of silence was broken, this time by Clarkson. He looked pleadingly at Wes.

"Well, you can't go now and leave this traitor defending us." He beckoned to Lisa. "I need you to stay with me."

Lisa snatched the vapo from Elwood's limp hand. She pumped the primer as she'd seen him do, and she got the weapon to whine to life as if she'd done it all the time. She rounded on Clarkson.

"I quit hours ago, asshole. Go to hell. I'm sure you can find the directions around here somewhere." Then she turned on Elwood. "And his name's *Wes*. Remember that next time," she hissed. She joined Wes at the door.

"Open up. We're going to save my kids."

"Looks clear." Dillon slid back behind a low decorative wall, but didn't give any sign she was ready to run.

Anna, Jenna and Kyle were crouched with her and had both been silent as they crept through the park. She recognized shock when she saw it. Years of extreme acts of animal liberation had put her in many dangerous situations, but this one was testing her reserves.

She indicated Kyle should lead the way. "Go."

"Not me. No way. You go first."

He now suspected she'd been using him as a canary. Being the leader of the group, she reasoned that they needed her alive. Anna was the only one who knew which substation to lead them to, and Jenna was a little too switched on to fall for it, which meant Kyle had drawn the short straw. Plus, even in shock, he and Anna had been subtly flirting, and that had irritated her more than anything.

"Kyle, we don't have time for this." She turned to Anna. "Are you sure this is the right way?"

Anna peeked over the wall. The new section was designed for younger children and had a variety of traditional rides: bumper cars, a small Ferris wheel with goblin-headed cars, a tilt-a-whirl, and a carousel of cartoon phantoms. She pointed to a branching road across from them.

"Down there is an open food court. A paddock of something. Then the substation that controls the west wall. That's the area Marv was supposed to be covering."

"Good. We can do this, guys."

Kyle closed his eyes and shook his head. On the way here, they had passed more ravaged bodies. With each step, his resolved had weakened.

"We should hide and stay put." He was trembling so much that the words were barely comprehendible.

Dillon sucked in an angry retort. She fought to stay calm. "It's too late for that. We're trapped in the cage with them. What do you think is going to happen if we just sit and do nothing?"

Kyle gave a humorless laugh. "That's you all over, ain't it, Sarah? You've just gotta do the right thing. Well, no. The right thing is to sit this out. I put this mission together too, remember? I know what the park's operational procedures are. And when the SkyShield goes up, there's a small unit at McCarran who comes riding in to open the gates to let us out."

Jenna was suddenly hopeful. "Is that true?"

"Absolutely. Right now, they're out there connecting the wall to the main grid. Then they'll open the gates. All we have to do is sit and wait."

Jenna gave a relieved chuckle.

"Of course, that's failure to execute," said Dillon, staring at the sky above.

"What does it matter?" said Anna. "We got them out. We made a statement. We've drawn the eyes of the world to what's going on here."

"Really? I don't think so. This will all blow over as some corporate accident. It'll be reopened in no time." She circled a finger in the air. "And all these critters will be back in their cages. With the shield up, they can't apport back to their own dimension. They're still stuck here. And we've accomplished nothing."

Kyle stared hard at her. "You have a major malfunction in your head, Sarah. You know that? What the hell happened to you?"

He shivered again when she met his gaze. Her face was placid, devoid of emotion. In the red hued light, her eyes seemed almost as dead as the pan-creatures they had risked their lives to defend.

"I was an army brat," she confided. "South Korea, Europe, back here. My pop drilled discipline in me night and day. He was an abusive son of a gun. I mean up here," she tapped her head for clarity. "He enjoyed screwing with everybody's mind. Drove my mum to try to run away. He found her. Wouldn't let her go. So she killed herself."

Kyle looked away. He already regretted asking her. But she wasn't finished.

"I was thirteen when that happened. And even after that, he just carried on. One day, he took me on a hunt. He knew I loved animals. So he took me on a bear hunt." She leaned her head against the wall, recalling the moment with vivid clarity. "We found a momma bear looking after her cub. I pleaded with my pop. But he just shot it. Boom." She mimed firing a rifle. "The cub ran. I often thought about it. What had happened to it? Could it survive on its own? Was it hunted down, or did it grow up and learn to hate man? All because of my pop. I swore from that point, to fight for the little guy. And those little guys are currently the animals around us, that we have temerity to think we rule over."

She stood, exposing herself to any predator in the plaza. Her confidence was unshakable.

"So sit here and pretend you're at the top of the food chain. You'll just discover that you're nothing but chowder." She vaulted the wall and looked back at them. "Oh, and your little story about the McCarran relief team. They're not coming. When I went out for the supplies yesterday, I wired their hangar. It would have gone off the moment they opened the door."

With her forearm, she wiped the sweat from her brow and slowly walked towards the road Anna had indicated to.

She didn't look back, but heard them emerge from cover and reluctantly follow her.

She was secretly relieved. She could sound as cocky as she liked, but she knew she couldn't complete her crusade on her own. She just hoped they wouldn't realize that.

Chapter 19

Wes didn't know where his energy reserves were coming from. He and Lisa had left the hub at a run, but less than fifty yards later, the sweltering heat had slowed them to a walking pace. It was hotter than it had been in the day, and Wes suspected the SkyShield was not only keeping any breeze out, but trapping heat in and simmering them. It'd been up for several hours now. He glanced at his watch. The screen on his cheap Casio was smashed. He searched his memory for how long containment procedures should last, but couldn't recall anything useful. He doubted that outside help was ever going to come.

Despite the physical punishment, there was no time to waste. They had to take the most direct path to the Enclave, which meant going off-road. From the air, the park's street network was subtly curved, like draped octopus tentacles, so they were not the quickest routes. Going off-road also meant they would have to traverse directly through some of the more worrisome attractions.

Wes didn't want to think about that right now.

"Thanks." They were the first words Lisa had spoken since leaving.

It was Wes' fault they were trapped in the Enclave. His fault that Lisa had brought them here. He couldn't think of a single thing she could be thankful for.

"No problem," was the only mumbling response he could think of. He noticed she kept nervously looking around. "Specters don't hang around."

It looked as if a riot had taken place in the street. Every window was broken, the sidewalks strewn with torn plush toys and cheap souvenir junk. A bookstore had been ransacked. Just to be cautious, he gave the dark entrance to a cinema – its entrance sculpted into an enormous maw – a wide berth. The darkness inside looked too thick, almost artificial. And he knew there were some phantoms that wove darkness like a spider weaves a web.

"It's funny how in the year and a half we've lived next door, you've been there more for Sean and Emma than their own father." She shook her head sadly. "Then again, Elwood's been there more than he has."

"That's what friends are supposed to do..." he said quietly, instantly regretting how lame that sounded. He knew any compliment she was about to give was purely a response to him volunteering to rescue her children. It was maternal gratitude, and he reminded himself not to think of it as anything more. This experience was hardening his resolve; forcing him to see things for what they really were. Tobias Elwood's weeping confession had done nothing more than confirm his choice to leave the park, to leave Nevada, was the right one.

"You never talked about him."

"There's nothing to tell." She clearly would not say anymore.

Sean had. Sean had told him everything one night when he found to kid crying on the garden swing after arguing with his mom. He'd complained about how Lisa never paid them much attention. Wes had sympathized, but he could also see the problems of adulthood went over the kid's head. A single mother in a job she hated, struggling to make ends meet and sacrificing her own happiness to do so. It had made Wes thankful he hadn't had children.

And yet…

Sean and Emma had turned into the best friends he had. Even during their tantrums, they were fun to be with. He suddenly realized *why* he was out here risking his life. It wasn't to impress the woman he had fallen for like a sucker; it was to rescue his friends. Suddenly, the knot of self-loathing he'd been harboring slackened as it was replaced by determination, and a silent thanks that he wasn't as shallow as Elwood.

Lisa suddenly squealed as an ectoplasm-soaked, cuddly phantom rebounded from her head. She spun the vapo around – slamming the barrel against Wes' ribs – but saw nothing.

"Hold your fire!" hissed Wes.

In the remains of a store filled with cuddly toys, they saw movement and heard childish tittering that sent chills through them. Vividly colored plush phantoms bobbed and weaved through the air before being slung at them. Wes batted aside a plush Angel of Death, wondering what the marketing department had been thinking of when they approved *that*.

Confused, Lisa asked, "What are they?"

"Poltergeist." Wes slipped a pair of yellow wrap-around shades off his head. They were heavy and uncomfortable and kept slipping down his nose. The augmented reality display showed the invisible blobs scampering around, picking up toys to play with, before hurling them at the humans. "I hate these guys."

As they left the bunker, Wes had stopped at an unopened emergency cache, taking everything that would fit in his pockets. He'd taken a taser, strapping the holster to his belt. A Tesla net hung from the back of his trousers. He was happy he hadn't left the shades behind.

"Do we run?"

Wes shook his head. "They'll just follow. Once they latch on to you, they follow from house to house." Lisa gripped her gun, ready to shoot. "And that thing'll just piss them off."

A chunk of broken window frame was chucked at them. They easily sidestepped it, but it wouldn't take long for the poltergeist to work their way up to more dangerous projectiles. A cash register and more damp plush toys were hurled with increasing fury.

Wes and Lisa backed away, which only encouraged the poltergeist to advance. Larger chunks of broken frames and wire display baskets crashed around them.

"Get behind me," Wes instructed as he pressed the stock of his vapo against his shoulder and sighted down the barrel.

"I thought you said that wouldn't work?"

Jagged shards of plate glass rose in the air – then were pelted towards them. They fell short, shattering on the ground, but it was only a matter of time before the poltergeist found their range. Wes stepped backwards, shielding Lisa and enticing the critters forward.

Closer... closer...

One pane of glass struck his leg, shattering in two, tearing his trousers and drawing blood. He just about battered aside a Phantom Land coffee mug aimed at his head. The poltergeist erupted into laughter.

"You little sons-of-puke," he hissed. Then fired.

He wasn't aiming at the pans – but the yellow fire hydrant on the sidewalk in front of the store. The ion flow shattered the concrete at its base. Weakened, the water pressure suddenly shot the hydrant high in the air – sending a cascade of water across the store and down the street.

And the poltergeist.

They howled and screamed as the liquid burned them. Even without the benefit of the shades, Lisa could now see the vague forms of the poltergeist highlighted by the dripping water. It ruptured them like a ripe cantaloupe. Their invisible carcasses dropped to the floor, splattering in a mass of ectoplasm that was sluiced away.

Wes gave Lisa a gentle nudge onwards.

"That way." He nodded towards a small access road between two buildings. The gate that would ordinarily keep guests out had been torn off its hinges.

"How far?"

"We're cutting through some ornamental gardens. Then... then we're close."

He caught the small spark of relief on Lisa's face.

It made him guilty for not telling her what the obstacle was *after* the gardens. She'd find that out soon enough.

Emma pressed herself further into the corner. Balled as

tightly as she could, she clasped her hands tightly over her ears to blot out the voice.

"I can still hear it!"

She saw Sean's lips move but heard nothing. She pulled her hands away.

"What?"

"I said it speaks in your mind. You don't need your ears."

They talked in low whispers. Sean was pushed next to her in the darkest corner they could find, which was a nook in the wall where a touch screen monitored the room. The graphs monitoring Raudive Waves peaked into the red. Ambient temperature and moisture readings were climbing, too. The only graph that remained green was the power flowing to the Tesla shield.

They had considered running, but a brief wave of frantic screaming from outside the tram entrance put them off. Even being near the Reaper made them feel sick, and the waves of fear had turned their legs to jello. They couldn't run away if they tried.

"Rrreelllaassee meeee…" crooned the voice in their head.

The huge mass behind the screen had stopped moving and hung in front of them. A pair of blazing red lupine eyes appeared on the dark figure, and it patiently watched them.

"No!" Sean shouted in defiance. "Go away!" He noticed Emma was staring back at the beast. "Don't look at it. Ignore it."

"It won't let us leave," she whispered, averting her eyes.

"Mom will come soon. She'll come and get us out of here."

"Nnnooobboooddyyy isssss coooominggg…" came the hissed response.

"Shut up!" snapped Sean. He turned Emma's face away, so that she was looking at him.

"Mommy won't come," she said.

Sean wasn't sure if the Reaper was influencing her, or if that's how she felt. Both were just as likely. Another batch of anguished screams came from outside; this time from the tram exit tunnel. Sean could imagine people running for their lives, but even facing imminent death, their primal instinct would prevent them from running in here for safety.

"Ttthhheeey cooomiiing foooorrrr yoooou," purred the Reaper. "I caaaannn heeellpp."

Sean gripped Emma's arm tighter. "Don't listen to it, Em. He's just trying to scare us. Mom *will* come, because Elwood is with her." Her eyes widened. Sean forced a smile. "You saw him on TV, right? Egypt, remember?" He pointed at the Reaper. "He shot that thing up so badly that it was squealing like a pig."

Despite her fear, Emma giggled. The Reaper hissed in retaliation. Sean forced a bigger smile.

"And that's why it's behind the screen begging to get out. Because it can't. That's why we're safe here. Tobias Elwood is going to save us, and we're going to be on TV talking about it. You're going to be famous!"

Emma's smile broadened.

The Reaper howled in fury, throwing itself against the screen. Sparks popped and crackled. The smell of ozone and charred flesh grew with the violent outburst. It was so frightening that Sean and Emma tried to shove themselves further into the corner, as the faint hope they had been experiencing was extinguished once again.

Chapter 20

Fog hung heavy in the air as Wes and Lisa walked beneath a rusting iron sign declaring they were entering LOVE-CRAFT GARDENS.

The atmospheric park was sculpted with trees that looked ready to mug the guests. Rocks and ancient-looking stone figures were carved into twisted monstrosities and eye-watering optical illusions. The air was a thick mist caused by the increasingly cloying atmosphere. Since walking from the shopping avenue, the temperature had incremented notice-ably. It was ridiculous to think they would run out of air, but Wes had never even considered if the SkyShield was *airtight*, and he wondered if the designers had even explored that. But there could be no doubt it was now trapping heat like a greenhouse. Again, he was certain that none of the park's engineers had ever thought about the prolonged effects of being trapped inside. He feared they had only a couple of hours before they dropped from heat exhaustion.

They circled around a huge stone fountain that had a stone tentacle-headed Elder God rising from the bowl.

Enormous hands were poised on the rim to pull it out. The water may have stopped flowing, but the haze added a sinister element to the sculpture.

"This doesn't look too bad."

Wes indicated to the left. "The Ghoul Enclosure is over there. That's a bad place to hang out." He gestured to the right. "The Wraith Stockade is that way. That's worse. If you want my opinion, we've got out of this lightly."

He caught the peculiar look she was giving him. If he didn't know better, it was one of newfound respect.

"Why is it I've never seen you bring a girlfriend back home?"

The question struck Wes from left field. "Um… what?"

"I just thought it was odd. That's all. I guessed you were married to your job. And I can see now what that means."

Wes remained tactfully silent.

"I'm kinda puzzled why you lied to me about what you do."

Wes stared at his feet as he walked. "You mean, why did I lie about shoveling ectoplasm all day? Why did I try to make myself look like I was somehow associated with the biggest heartthrob on TV?" He shook his head. "Let me think. That's a toughie…"

Lisa gave the smallest of laughs and leaned closer to him. "I get it. It's kinda lame. It's just as bad as being a thirty-something single mom who's chose the worst time to pick gift bags." After a contemplative beat, she added, "Sean and Emma were always baffled."

"About what? Why they lived next door to the single loner serial liar?"

"Why you never asked me out on a date."

Wes is suddenly brought up short. His brain firing a thousand questions – which were silenced by the close sound of sobbing. He traced the business end of his vapo towards it.

Lisa's head bobbed as she tried to locate its source. "There," she whispered, pointing into the mist.

Wes stepped in front of her. "Careful, they had boggarts and Will-o'-the-wisps in here. They're only Class I, but as mischievous as hell."

They edged closer. A shadow sat on a park bench, its head cradled in its hands as it wailed.

"Is that one?" whispered Lisa.

Wes shook his head, unsure. Some spooks had the power of mimicry down to a fine art to lure their victims. He pumped the vapo, and it whined to life – getting the attention of the figure. Its head shot up.

"Who's there?" came a thick Welsh accent.

Wes stepped closer to see it was a park technician. His uniform was torn and splattered in blood. His eyes were bloodshot. He held up his hands when he saw the gun.

"Shoot me now. Get it over with!"

Wes lowered the weapon. "I'm not gonna shoot you. What are you doing out here?"

"I didn't mean to do it. I just didn't," the Welshman sobbed, placing his head back in his hands.

"Do what?"

"I had a voice in here." He tapped his head. "It told me. Begged me to change those timers… I thought it was the right thing to do. I really did…"

"You're one of the terrorists!"

The man looked up, aghast. "Terrorist? Are you out of your mind? I'm a bloody freedom fighter, I am. A liberator."

Lisa stepped forward. "You caused all of this?"

"Not on me own, no. But–"

She slugged him hard across the face. The man recoiled,

hands raised for protection, as she swung again. So much for his death wish. Wes tossed the vapo over his shoulder and grabbed Lisa around the waist, pulling her back before the blow could connect.

"My children could die because of you! You bastard!"

The man pulled his feet onto the bench and curled up defensively.

"They were supposed to go off when it'd had closed! I swear to God! This wasn't supposed to happen!"

"Well, it has! Because of you!"

Lisa struggled from Wes's hold. The fleeting moment of tenderness between them had vanished. That was the second reason Wes could think of for shooting the Brit.

"It showed me terrible things," he cried. "I had to do it…"

Wes's eyes narrowed as he understood. "The Reaper?"

"Yes. I was only in there for minutes and it got into my head. Told me awful things…" he muttered.

Lisa couldn't hold back her anguish. "That's where my children are!" She gripped Wes's arm. "What will it do to them?"

"Nothing. Sshh, easy. They're kids. They're not as susceptible to the Raudive voices. They can handle it far better than we can." While that was true, there was no hard data on how long that resistance lasted. "We're close, Lisa. Really close. I need you to keep it together."

Remarkably, she calmed and nodded, but threw a black look at the Welshman.

"We only wanted them to be free," he wailed. "They didn't deserve to be cooped up in cages."

"Free?" barked Wes. "These aren't ordinary animals. They don't belong here – and I don't mean in the park. They don't belong in our *dimension*. Do you understand?

They're an invasive species. Interlopers, phasing through to feed from our fear. Theirs is a very different world. Have you ever seen what happens when an invasive species is introduced into an ecosystem? It never goes well."

"They told me ghosts had rights too. And I believed them." He gave a thousand-yard stare into the mist. "I just wanted them gone. They cost me everything. Me wife, me business... I lost it all."

"Because you're a complete moron," Lisa snarled.

He focused on her with pleading eyes. "I thought they were more like something out of the cartoons. I swear I thought we were doing the right thing," he repeated with less conviction than before.

"They're interdimensional trans-phase beings with a taste for human flesh and misery," said Wes. "You weren't doing the right thing." He waved his hands. "None of this is the right thing."

"Sorry..." the man's voice broke.

Lisa walked away. "I don't have time to listen to your self-pity."

"Let me help." The man jumped to his feet. "Your children. Let me help find them."

Lisa's eyes narrowed. "Why would I possibly trust you?"

"I got nothing to live for, do I? If I get out of this alive, then they'll arrest me and throw away the key."

"I doubt it. Nevada still has the death penalty."

"Exactly." The man extended his hand. "I'm Mike. Let me make this right."

Lisa and Wes looked at his outstretched hand but made no motion to take it.

"Okay," said Wes as he followed Lisa. "You can tag along. But don't think for a second we're going to waste any time saving your butt."

Mike nodded and followed. Lisa gave Wes a sidelong look. He was lost in his own personal dilemma, wondering what Tobias Elwood would do in a situation like this. Probably turn and run, he concluded.

The mist gave no sign of thinning as they reached broad stone steps leading up a slope. At the top was a huge gothic mansion that looked as if it had been transplanted straight from New England. Every wall, tower, and crenelation was at an angle. It exuded malice.

Lisa gasped in consternation. "What now?"

"Every good theme park has one," said Wes and he unslung his vapo. "A haunted house. Only this one really is haunted."

Chapter 21

Sophie was leaning back in her chair, with her feet up on the desk, and massaging a cold Pepsi can against her forehead, when she noticed the blinking light on her monitoring station. She snapped upright and double-tapped the screen.

"Guys! We have a temperature warning."

The temperature in the room was slowly rising despite the air con. Listening to the whirl of the unit over the last few minutes had confirmed to everybody that it was barely drawing power.

"We know it's hot in here," said Hugh, fanning himself with an iPad. "I don't need the computer to tell me that."

"No. I mean the external environmental monitors."

Blake stepped behind her so he could see the map on her screen. All the zones across the park were flashing a deep orange. Temperature fluctuations didn't appear to affect the exhibits, but they could really affect the guests and machinery. Cooling sprinkler systems were positioned everywhere to help regulate the crowds. They might not be able to see the guests anymore, but they had to be out there somewhere.

Blake just hoped they were still alive.

"Jeez. It's one-hundred four out there. The shield is generating a lot of heat."

"Can we leech power from somewhere and activate the sprays?"

"From where? We don't have a single amp to spare. Besides, the sprays take up more power than the cameras, so we can't copy that trick. I'm more worried about the electrical systems. If they overheat…"

She called up the SkyShield interface as Tanaka, Hugh, Scott and Ying gathered around her to watch. Clarkson, Ralph, and Becky sat on the floor drinking cold sodas from the refrigerator and lacked the energy to move. Elwood was slumped in the corner, away from the others. He hadn't spoken since Wes left.

"It must be that hot in here," Clarkson grumbled.

"It's sixty-nine in here. And that's with the air con on," Sophie said. The schematics of the perimeter wall appeared. Every Tesla tower was green, indicating it was working, but the temperatures were riding high. "Look at that. Even if the external team opens the gates, it's going to be like running through a furnace."

"The Shield wasn't built to run this long," Blake said grimly. "Why aren't we getting any overheating alarms?"

"It looks like the relays shorted."

Blake stroked his chin as he thought through the ramifications. "If the relays are popping, then we're getting incorrect sensor readings… or the sensors are bust."

"Likely," said Sophie. She looked at him with concern when she realized what he was driving at. "You're wondering what other critical systems aren't working?"

Tanaka groaned as he understood. "Christ! Half the park could be in meltdown, and we wouldn't know from in here!"

The main screens suddenly went dark, leaving only the emergency lighting. The crew rushed to their stations. Hugh was already examining the substations' output.

"I have temperature alarms in both substations," he reported. "The cooling systems have failed."

"How long until we lose them?" asked Blake.

"I just have the alarms. I don't have data."

Clarkson forced himself to sit upright. He winced as pain throbbed through his leg. "What does that mean for the shield?"

"The shield will run off a single substation. But if we lose the other, we lose this room and anything else that was working out there."

"That doesn't sound fantastic for us."

Blake kept his eyes on Sophie's screen as she cycled through other sensor readings, trying to get further informa-tion. "No, it's not. It means we either sit here in the dark and slowly bake to death. Or we take our chances outside."

The emergency lights chose that moment to flicker. Everybody traded concerned looks. Elwood climbed to his feet, noticing the screens were down.

"How long before a rescue team arrives?" he said.

Blake shot him a look loaded with disappointment. "They should've arrived in the first thirty minutes. Some-thing's gone critically wrong."

Elwood darted to his side. "What?"

"How do I know?" Blake tried not to shout, but he was having difficulty controlling his temper. "Maybe they can't connect to an external power-feed? Unless the whole of Vegas is in a blackout? Maybe they're stuck in traffic? Right now, we're at Plan-B." He took some satisfaction in seeing Elwood's brow knit in confusion.

"What's Plan-B?"

"Plan-B is that we sit, wait, and hope that somebody outside comes up with a Plan-C."

The lights flickered again. Tanaka suddenly howled and swiped an open palm at the side of his monitor.

"My console's dead!"

Ralph became aware the asthmatic gasp from the air conditioning had stopped. He stood on his tiptoes and held a hand in front of the vent.

"It's dead."

"There must be a way to lessen the load," said Hugh with growing desperation.

Now everybody except Clarkson was on their feet, eager to do something to help.

"Show me the Enclave," Blake instructed.

Hugh called up the plan. It indicated that the shields were up, but little else.

Blake breathed out heavily. "That's something, at least."

Elwood leaned close. "You know, there's a simple way of fixing this. Turn the SkyShield off." Blake looked at him as if he were crazy. Elwood held up a finger to stop him from interrupting. "We'd still have the power in here."

"And what about everybody else?"

"It would give people the chance to run like hell. And with the roof down, we'd get some cooler air in."

Sophie shook her head. "There was no breeze forecast tonight. Maybe it'd lower the temperature a fraction... I'm not sure. Thermodynamics isn't my field of expertise."

Blake thrust a forefinger against Elwood's solid chest. "And we'd have every spook rushing for the exits."

"They're not sprinters, Blake. Sure, we might lose a few

if they got out, but with nothing keeping them here, they might apport back to their own dimension, with any luck. And it would give people a chance. And the Enclave will still be powered."

For a moment, Blake saw the fractured logic. Then he dismissed it.

"Whatever the death toll is in here, whatever gets out there will bring Vegas to its knees. Even if it's a half dozen phantoms."

"We can turn the shield back on after a few minutes. It would still contain a majority of them," Elwood insisted.

"You're assuming we'll be able to turn it back on," said Tanaka grimly. "I can't see that happening. We're on a downhill slope. If the SkyShield comes down, it's going to stay down. And if we try to crank it up again, these systems are so shot, it's likely that it will just keel over completely."

Elwood shrugged. "Which means what?"

"It means we lose this room, too. We lose the shield. And we lose all power to the Enclave. We lose the park."

They silently absorbed that.

Then the power in the room went completely out.

It was like walking back in time. The splendid entrance hall was dominated by a pair of staircases sweeping upwards and branching either side of the hall, eventually reaching either end of a grandiose first floor landing. A huge organ took up one wall. Normally, it would play mournful tunes as intrepid guests entered, but without power, it was silent. Disturbing pictures of fictitious ex-residents hung on the wall. Their eyes followed guests because of ingenious holographic projection – an effect which was again lost. Instead, the portraits gazed out with hollow eye sockets, which was far more unsettling.

Wes and Lisa swept their flashlights across the mock antique furnishings. The imposed darkness added yet another layer of menace that was absent when the attraction was functioning. Mike kept uncomfortably close to them, breathing down their ears.

"Reminds me of my old place back in Wales. Before you lot put me out of business." He had related his personal woes as they entered the mansion, but all it had done was further alienate Lisa's sympathies from the man. "Which means I can tell you for sure that coming in here is a bloody stupid idea."

Lisa hated agreeing with him. Wes caught her pleading look.

"This is the quickest route. At the back of this is Terror Boulevard and a maintenance road that cuts straight across to the Enclave. It saves a two-mile round trip if we stuck to the streets." He indicated to the staircase. "We go up."

The sprawling mansion felt like a maze, with twisting corridors that enticed guests through a string of themed rooms, accumulating in a lavish ballroom. Leading thousands of people into a dead-end was impractical for a theme park attraction, so guests were often unaware there were four routes through the house, each identical, ending in four ballrooms. It was designed for optimum traffic flow, but exploring families often found themselves split, leading to the bizarre feeling of sharing the same experience at the same time – just not together. It was a simple secret, but guests often wondered if they had been trapped in some sort of time loop – something the park was eager to promote.

Wes led the way up the staircase. The Stygian darkness could conceal anything, and the flashlights cast their own jumping shadows on the walls, but at least it was cooler than outside, which buoyed their flagging strength.

"We keep the Corpulent Phantoms here. They don't like to move, so I'm guessing they're still in residence."

Lisa's knuckles were already white from gripping the gun. "They sound charming."

"Actually, their bark is worse than their bite. A lot of noise and ectoplasm, but guests can touch them without getting their hands bitten off." Wes wasn't afraid of the regular residents. He was afraid of what had moved in when the fences went down.

This wasn't on his usual work roster, so he had only been through twice, but he was aware the rule was to keep moving forward to get out. He indicated they take the left-hand branching corridor; it looked just as ominous as the other.

With each step, shadows bobbed across the walls, making it difficult to judge what was ahead. A sharp corner led deeper into the mansion, offering a prime ambush point. Wes motioned for the others to stay behind him. His courage was drawn by his overwhelming desire to get out of the house.

He edged around the corner, pressing against the far wall and keeping the vapo raised and ready to fire, as he had seen Tobias Elwood do in so many episodes of Spook Hunters. The flashlight beam cut straight down the corridor.

"Oh, boy."

The others joined him. The occasions when Wes had

been through the house, the park had been closed and the attraction was powered down. Only now did he remember some of the more physical challenges ahead.

The interior had been designed with no right angles. Everything was slightly off-kilter, giving the illusion that even perfectly level floors were slanted. Guests would often stagger, as if seasick. The next hundred yards of corridor took that to the extreme. The entire passage corkscrewed a full three-hundred sixty degrees. Had the hydraulic system been activated, the corridor would slowly buckle and twisted, giving the effect they were walking down some monstrous gullet. They couldn't ignore the few bodies that had been cast around. One was wedged on the underside of a table that now hung from the ceiling. Blood still dripped from it. Another was wedged between a display cabinet and a suit of armor. The back of their skull had been bitten off.

"I thought you said Corpulent Phantoms weren't dangerous?"

Wes licked his lips as he warily stepped onto the sloping floor. "Yeah. I'm only worried about the neighbors."

Lisa struggled to keep her vapo's flashlight illuminating the floor ahead of her as she climbed over an antique trophy cabinet that stretched horizontally across the wall-cum-floor. Its reinforced glass doors were slick with blood and ectoplasm. She ignored Mike's offered helping hand.

Wes continued on without looking back. "Confined walls. Plenty of spaces to hide. There're a lot of pans who'd thrive here."

Mike brought up the rear. He slipped on the goo, but caught his balance. Hopping off the cabinet, he then had to duck under a table bolted in the middle of the floor that had orbited around to become the wall. It was like walking through an Escher painting.

A low chittering noise suddenly echoed from the end of the corridor. Wes stopped, bracing himself on a forty-five-degree sloping portion of the ceiling. He crouched slightly behind the chandelier a couple of yards ahead that poked from the floor like a crystal mushroom. The noise started again, echoing from the irregular surface, so it sounded as if it was coming from everywhere.

Mike's frightened whisper was so close behind that it made Wes jump.

"What is that?"

"Something's just trying to scare us."

"It's doing a bloody good job."

It was doing an *excellent* job, Wes thought. He recognized the call. The creature was a master at conjuring fear. He powered the vapo down and slung it over his shoulder. It was useless. Keeping his flashlight scanning the shadows, he drew the taser from its holster.

Lisa frowned. "What is it?"

"When you were a kid, did you ever think there was something under the stairs? Or something lurking in your closet?"

"Uh-huh."

Wes lowered his voice. "That's because there was."

"You're talking about the Bogeyman?"

Wes shook his head and checked the taser was on. A flashing green LED assured him it was fully charged.

"Something far worse," he whispered.

Nobody moved. They held their collective breath and peered into the darkness ahead. They were only yards from a T-junction and the next step to freedom.

Nothing stirred.

Wes was about to step forward when another faint chitter froze him in place. It had taken him far too long to recognize the distinctive striated wounds on the victims behind them. And now he had, he regretted bringing them through here.

He also remembered the creature was a master of ambush. Often projecting its calls to keep a victim frozen on the spot...

Wes tracked his flashlight straight up.

The floor was above them, with a pair of wingback leather armchairs bolted in place and lending a vertiginous air to the view. From the dark recesses between two enormous bookcases, a long arm was reaching down. Its four-foot grasp was extended by foot-long slender taloned fingers. The sinewy skin glistened like fleshy bones and gave it its common folklore name: *Bloody-Bones*. Its ovoid head emerged from the darkness. Beady red eyes sat over a wide Cheshire Cat smile – although only if the cat was frothing at the mouth and its jaws were lined with thousands of pin sharp teeth. The skin was taut, wet, and blood red. A feature that gave it its more common name:

"A Raw-Head!" Wes gasped. A cousin of the Bogeyman, it lacked the shape changing ability, but replaced it with a pathological bloodlust. "RUN!"

Wes leaped from the cabinet and attempted a tuck-and-roll as he'd seen Elwood do so many times. The tilted floor pitched him at an angle, and he crashed into another suit of armor laying across the wall-cum-floor. Lisa accidentally kicked him in the back as she tripped over him, and he heard a clatter as she sprawled in the darkness.

With the only two light sources skittering across the floor ahead, Mike was now a perfect target for the Raw-Head. The claws wrapped around his neck and yanked him upwards with a choked cry.

Wes groped in the darkness for the taser – and saw the

green LED blinking feet away at the bottom of the sloping wall. He crawled over the armor. The confused geography of the inverted passage was making his head spin.

Lisa landed on her vapo, the steel crushing the wind from her. She rolled onto her back and saw Mike's legs kicking overhead as he was pulled towards a widening maw. With a howl, she pulled the trigger and unleashed the ion stream. The inverted table the Raw-head was using as a perch splintered in the maelstrom. It plummeted – along with Mike – to the floor. It shattered the crystal chandelier, casting shards of safety glass in every direction.

Lisa rolled to her feet, casting the vapo's flashlight over the destruction. Mike had rebounded from the table and was clambering to his feet. His right arm hung limply, forcing him to cradle it with the other. From the shattered chandelier, the Raw-Head sprung up like a jack in the box. Its slender humanoid body was essentially skinless. The bones and pulsing internal organs were clearly visible beneath a translucent red ectoplasmic layer. It towered over Mike, issuing a distinctive chittering. Neither the fall nor the ion blast seemed to have caused any harm. Lisa fired again anyway.

The energy stream struck the creature, preventing it from pouncing on Mike. It staggered several steps back from the impact, but was otherwise unhurt. The Welshman ran. Lisa turned and ran with him towards Wes, who had just retrieved the taser.

The Raw-Head agilely sprung onto the acutely sloping wall and hung there like a spider.

"Come on!" Wes waved ahead.

The trio ran for their lives, hopping over items that should be rightfully on walls, and vaulting over furniture as the geography around them began to normalize. They reached the T-junction. A quick glance behind showed the Raw-Head springing from the wall-to-ceiling-to-wall as it spiraled around to give chase.

Wes's boot, slick with gore, sent him skidding at the junction as he took the branching left corridor. He slammed hard into the wall, but continued running. A doorway led into a dark bedroom. Heavily decorated with curtains and a stately four-poster bed that provided amble opportunity for the local phantoms to hide and spring out on guests. They didn't stop.

They reached the far exit when a terrible clatter rose from behind. The Raw-Head had jumped on top of the bed's canopy, which broke under its weight, sending it crashing to the mattress. Lisa paused long enough to fire another ion volley behind them. The broken canopy, bedsheets, and once dangling curtains instantly caught fire. The beast howled and crawled from the flames, smoke rising from its flanks. It looked injured. Apparently, it didn't like fire. Lisa turned and ran.

At another right-angled corner, Wes didn't even slow down, reasoning that whatever was around the corner couldn't be worse than what was pursuing them.

His flashlight revealed another room: a spacious Victorian-style kitchen. Lethal looking knives and cleavers hung from the walls and worktops. There were three bodies here. Guests who had been ripped apart as they had taken the knives for defense, before realizing they were plastic replicas, seconds before they were killed. The gruesome sight didn't slow Wes, and a small voice at the back of his mind worried that he was becoming too accustomed to gruesome death.

A wide doorway beckoned ahead. Another glance behind confirmed Lisa and Mike were keeping close and the

Raw-Head was restlessly pursuing, but its injuries had slowed it. There was now a chance to out-run it.

Wes shouldered through the double doors, and they entered a spacious ballroom. His flashlight slashed through the darkness. During normal operations, concealed Tesla fences would deflect Corpulent Phantoms to congregate here, where, along with actors, guests could 'waltz with the dead'. Huge chandeliers adorned the ceiling with a massive ghostly mosaic running around the walls.

The exit door was straight ahead.

Three glowing blobs appeared in front of them. Each the size of an armchair, the Corpulent Phantoms represented their namesake, hovering from the waist up like grotesquely fat men with their squat, neckless, domed heads pushed into their shoulders. They flailed at the humans with stubby fat arms.

Lisa was running so fast that she ran straight into one. Ectoplasm splattered across her as she *ran through* the phantom, emerging on the other side, whimpering but unharmed. The low-class phantoms had trouble making physical contact with people, which made them the ideal occupants for the house.

She slipped on the ectoplasm and sprawled face first across the parquet floor. She reached for Mike as he passed.

"Help me up!"

Mike hesitated – then saw the Raw-Head had entered the room. He turned and fled for the exit. Lisa spat out the foul-tasting gunk and wiped it from her eyes.

"You bastard!" she yelled. She tried to stand, but her hands and feet slipped like a newborn calf trying to find its feet. She facepalmed the floor again.

And the Raw-Head was upon her.

She raised her hand to fend it off. The creature's wide mouth extended around her arm, ready to chomp.

With a guttural roar, Wes doubled-back and charged the Raw-Head with his taser pointed straight at it. He didn't trust his aim – if he missed, Lisa was dead. He felt the barrel press against the Raw-Head's skull, and he pulled the trigger.

The point-blank shot sent a numbing recoil through Wes's arm as the electrical charge blistered the Raw-head's skull. Wes was sent sprawling backwards across the floor.

The Raw-Head thrashed, groping at the section of its skull that had been blown away. Wes crabbed towards Lisa and helped her stand, before looking back to see six Corpulent Phantoms now surrounded the Raw-Head. They mobbed it, tearing into with half-starved choler. They may be harmless to humans, but that didn't mean they were harmless to other pan-species.

Wes and Lisa staggered for the exit as the mewing Raw-Head was pulled limb from limb.

Chapter 22

The push in the small of his back, sending him through to door was anything but subtle. Tobias Elwood stood several paces from the hub's open door and slowly turned around. He regretted giving Lisa his vapo. He was now an open target.

Blake emerged next. After shoving Elwood firmly out, he had waited to see if anything attacked. So far, so good. Steinberg and Ying carried Clarkson between them, followed by Ralph, Becky, Hugh and Tanaka. Sophie was the last out.

At night, the air was usually alive with screams, and during the day there was constant activity and staff announcements. The sizzle from the SkyShield was the only sound in the park.

Elwood kept his voice low as he looked around. "Which way?"

Hugh pointed north. "The substation is on the other side of the utility garage."

The moment the power had failed, Blake had grouped

them around the light of several shared cell phone screens. In the darkness, they were trapped and ineffective. Until they opened the door, they hadn't even been sure if it was just the power to the command hub that had been cut, or if the SkyShield was down too. It was some relief to see the phosphorous sky above them. The decision was made for them. Rather than suffocate in the darkness, they would head to the closest substation and attempt to manually restore power to the command hub. At first, the collective decision was that Elwood was the best choice for the suicide mission, until he pointed out that the garage housed several spook-proof transport trucks.

"You mean you cart those things around the world in the back of a cage?" Clarkson had asked incredulously.

"How do you think they get here?" Blake said dismissively.

Clarkson wasn't in the mood for an argument. A plan was fermenting. One that might see them all survive... or him, at least.

"If a phantom can't get out of them, then it can't get in either."

The mission to restart the power suddenly turned into an improvised escape plan. It was decided that, if the restart failed, then the next best thing would be to hide in the back of a transit container. That had lifted Elwood's spirits, and he had performed a volte-face, promising to return in one of the trucks to rescue them.

That had been the first time he had seen just how badly his reputation had suffered. Nobody had faith he'd keep to his word. That they'd rather take the risk and cross the park, rather than trust him, spoke volumes.

Between the abandoned hospital and the staff canteen, was a large prep area for the supernatural themed parades.

The colorful floats were still lined up, partially prepared for the special Halloween night parade. They had managed one tour before things had turned sour. As they passed, Elwood heard muttered gasps from the group as they spotted the bloodstains and torn chunks taken from the decorations.

Even with the soaring temperatures, Elwood felt cold. Worse, he felt a fraud.

In front of the TV cameras, he was alive and at ease. Whatever the terror was, he faced it with confidence, never losing the charming façade he had become known for. He'd been on countless chat shows around the world in which hosts marveled at his levelheadedness. Surveys had ranked him as *the* guy to have on your side in a crisis. And yet, when it came to the crunch, he knew it was all a show. Literally. Each Spook Hunter show involved hundreds of hours of meticulous planning with military tacticians, scientists, his fellow Spook Hunters, and the production team. The danger was real, but the preparation and hardware at their disposal mitigated it. Sure, people had died making the show. In fact, if there hadn't been a few deaths, then the ratings would have suffered.

Lying on his back in the command center and feeling waves of sympathy for himself, he had considered quitting. His reputation and career had been shattered. It would take a miracle to repair it. The only problem with quitting was giving up the rich vein of merchandise and lucrative TV contracts. Instead, he had formed a plan to contact his lawyers as soon as he had a phone signal and slam an NDA on everybody who had been in the bunker with him.

All he had to do was survive. He was good at that.

A glimpse of a yellow supply cache galvanized him. They had passed one torn from the wall, its contents plundered. This one was untouched. He pulled the panel down, taking the vapo, taser, and Tesla net for himself. It left nothing for the others, but they didn't appear too concerned.

Priming the weapon was like supercharging his manhood. The sense of unease and fear that had made him afraid was suddenly banished. He felt his old self return as he turned to the group.

"Okay, folks. We're five minutes out. Stick with me, I've got this covered."

"How can we be lost?" Dillon spat for the second time as Anna paused at a branch in the avenue.

"Everything looks different in the dark!" She hissed. "And there are no signs!"

The state-of-the-art park had relied on state-of-the-art tech, which meant park maps were huge touch screens, and even simple signs were digital. Even the icons on the washroom doors were tiny screens that looped animations.

"Think," Dillon said impatiently. Their progress had been cautious, and therefore slow. They had given a large group of guests a wide berth. They'd been hiding in an empty paddock. Jenna had argued they'd be safer in numbers. Dillon didn't need any hangers-on and had no time for small talk. She'd left Jenna with them and was relieved when Kyle and Anna continued on with her.

Five minutes later, they had taken cover in a drainage

ditch as a herd of wights trotted past, sniffing in the direction of the large group.

This new junction, like most others, was lined with snack bars. An Irish themed pub, *O'Scares*, lay opposite *Dr Macabre's Mansion of Madness*, which sold a range of prosthetic horror masks from both real life and the movies. Like every other place, the windows had been broken, and the stock ravaged. Many of the latex masks had been chewed to shreds. Anna imagined the map and used the shop as a reference point.

"I think it's this way." She pointed into the darkness.

"Are you sure?"

Anna hesitated. Then, "yes."

Dillon sighed. "The sooner we get there, the sooner we get out and all those folks back there," she jerked her thumb the way they had come, "will have a chance of survival. So pull yourself together!"

Anna nodded firmly. "I'm sure."

Dillon was about to speak to Kyle, but he was staring uneasily into the darkness. She joined him.

"Hey? What is it?"

Only when she got closer, could she make out a large black stone archway that blended with the darkness. Engraved in the stone was the attraction name: *The Bogeyman Tunnels*.

"When I was a kid, I was terrified of an old wardrobe in my bedroom."

"Your fashion sense, or…?"

Kyle's voice was a whisper. "It was an antique that had come over from Europe. It'd been in the family for generations. Nobody liked it, but nobody had the guts to toss it out. I was always convinced there was something in there. I'd wake up screaming. The door ajar. Something stirring in the darkness…"

"A Bogeyman." Dillon said. "Or Bogeywoman, there's got to be some, right? You never hear about them."

"I just remember how much it scared me. Of course, my dad told me not to be stupid. Said they didn't exist. But I kept believing. So he started beating me for lying." He gave a dark chuckled. "I can't ever remember seeing anything, but…"

"I read about them. They can fuzz up your memory. It's a survival trick." She wasn't looking at the entrance, she was studying his face. His youthful vigor that had been missing for the last few days had returned. She'd always been a loner. Life with her father had foisted it on her. She'd made a point of never getting involved with anybody in her activism groups after seeing how it inevitably led to problems and heartbreak when one or the other had been arrested. Yet there was something about Kyle's innocence that was drawing her to him. She hated that. And she hated how she felt every time he and Anna flirted.

"I got the crap beat out of every week because of those things. The little bastards tortured me every night. And now here we are, liberating them so they can hide under some kid's bed and scare the bejesus outta them."

"Some kids need to be scared. That's what keeps society in check. Come on." She gently tugged his elbow. A clattering from Dr Macabre's made them freeze and sharply reminded them they were weaponless. The shadows shifted inside… then a man staggered out.

"Nathan?" Dillon could hardly believe her eyes. "You're alive!"

Nathan nodded, but he looked dazed and confused. His uniform was ripped and bloodied. His hair wild and matted.

Anna hugged him tightly. "Is Marv with you?" She peered over his shoulder into the empty store.

Nathan shook his head and treated her to a haunted look.

"What happened to you?" Dillon said quietly. He was the shell of the man she'd known. She raised a hand. "Tell us later. I'm just glad you're alive. Stick close."

Feeling energized that the ordeal was nearly over, she began jogging towards the substation. "Come on. We're getting out of here."

Anna's recollection had been perfect. An eight-foot-tall hedge ran along the left-hand side of the road, obscuring the service buildings behind, including a hydro plant that powered the Rabid Rapids ride. Even in the dim SkyShield light, she located the narrow line in the hedge that delineated the hidden gate. With the help of Dillon and Kyle, they rolled it aside. Nathan kept in the shadows, looking cautiously around.

Passing through the gate, a short approach road ran straight to the substation. Beyond, they could see it opened up into a wider area: maintenance sheds, a workshop – in which several bodies were strewn, having tried to defend themselves with drills and buzz saws – and the park's fire station.

But Dillon only had one target. The substation. That was their ticket out of this nightmare.

Chapter 23

Against the raging sky, the Enclave pyramid had a touch of the apocalypse about it. Wes thought it was the sort of perfect photo the park's publicity team would fight for. But after tonight, he doubted there would be a park left.

"Do we all have to go in?" Mike asked feebly.

Lisa shot him a look. "We need nothing from a filthy coward like you. You left me to die back there."

"What could I do? I saw he had it covered." he pointed at Wes.

"Will you cut it out?" snapped Wes. They'd been bickering since they'd left the haunted house. While he entirely agreed with Lisa, he needed Mike on her side for the task ahead. His direct, if brief, experience with the Angel of Death could prove useful.

They were standing outside the tram entrance. The dark portal had no gate. There wasn't one that could contain the beast inside, and very few things had the desire to willingly enter. The moist air drifted out like a monstrous hot breath, ruffling their hair and knotting their stomachs in fear. The sense of being unwelcome was visceral.

Wes clung on to his vapo like a life preserver, although it would be nothing more than an irritant to the beast inside. "We go straight in and out. No heroics. Don't look at the Reaper. It will get into your head. You can't stop it, but don't focus on it. They're just words trying to manipulate you." He looked sidelong at Mike. "It can't control you. It only makes suggestions. If you do what it tells you to… that's on you. Are you ready?"

The last was aimed squarely at Lisa. Even with the light from the hellish sky, she still looked pale. Speckled with blood, dried ectoplasm, sweat, dust, and with her hair frazzled and wild. Yet she still made his heart skip a beat. This was the part in the movie when the hero kissed his love interest. He wanted to tell her how he felt. He wanted to unload all his feelings before he died. But the reality was that unloading his emotional baggage now would be the worst possible timing. All that really mattered was the children.

They'd go in. Out. Then he'd leave everything behind and never look back.

If he survived that long.

Lisa trembled as she gripped the vaporizer, but gave a single terse nod. Then, to his surprise, she led the way forward.

Condensation trickled from the ceiling and down the walls. Wes knew acutely that waterproofing sensitive electronics in the middle of the desert wasn't a primary safety feature anybody had thought of. In the red light that made it through the entrance, it looked like the walls were weeping blood.

The track curved to the right. The vapos' flashlights cut

through the fine mist and illuminated the titanic figures of death looming either side of them. Wes walked in lockstep with Lisa. He was surprised to hear involuntary squeals of terror from the Welshman who had followed them in. Wes would have bet hard cash that he would have bolted at the entrance. Perhaps he had more resolve than Wes gave him credit for.

A sense of terror tickled their minds, urging them to flee. The air became almost too hot and thick to breathe, yet they pressed forward. The track curved again, revealing the pulsing curved Tesla screen. Their eyes became so accustomed to the darkness that they could now make out the panels and conduits running along the opposite wall, and the open service door through which Sean and Emma had entered.

"Sean? Em?" Lisa didn't dare raise her voice above a stage whisper.

It was a struggle not to look at the pulsing screen. Just a few more steps and they were inside enough to spot the recess the children had been hiding in.

They weren't there.

Lisa gave a sob of despair.

The Tesla screen cracked and rippled, drawing their attention. The shadow of the Reaper hung in the center, like a giant black fetus. And below, to the side of the curved screen, were Sean and Emma. They tightly hugged one-another, sobbing so hard they were hyperventilating.

"Emma! Sean!" Lisa motioned them over. "Come here. Quick!"

They didn't move.

"Kids!" snapped Wes, desperate to stop his voice trembling. "Come here, right now!" He noticed the fire ax was embedded in the base of the energy screen just feet from them. The Reaper must have convinced them to hack it apart, not counting on frail strength of a child.

"They can't hear you," stuttered Mike. He was struggling to even look at the thing. He tapped a finger against his temple. "It gets in here. Whispers until you have no choice but to listen. You can't even hear your own thoughts." He met Wes's look. "It wants you to fetch them. It *wants* to kill you."

The burning smell from inside the substation made Dillon wretch. It was like walking into a putrid sauna. But at least the lights were on, even if everything was shaded by a mist hanging in the air. Or at least she thought it was mist. It could have been smoke. The transformer sounded unhealthy, issuing a deep throbbing noise that vibrated her ribcage. It was only a matter of time before it keeled over without her help.

"Look for the cutoff switch," she shouted over the discord. She glanced back to check the others were searching for it.

Kyle was suspended a foot off the ground by a shaggy, hairy claw. Anna had her back to him and hadn't yet seen what was happening. Dillon was about to warn Nathan… but then noticed the arm was Nathan's.

Or what she thought had been him.

Nathan's head was swelling and distorting, revealing cobalt scaled skin beneath. Even his clothing warped as it transformed back to fur. Dillon was transfixed. She had studied many of the pan-species before embarking on her crusade and recognized a Bogeyman when she saw one. A shape-shifting creature that used your memories as a weapon. It must have been lurking in Doctor Macabre's, detecting their mental imprints of Nathan.

"I think I've found it!" Lisa declared triumphantly. She pointed to a hefty lever on the wall. Then she saw Kyle – just as the Bogey's mouth hyper-extended, and it bit his face off. Teeth raked flesh from the skull, shattering his nose and pulling his jawbone off. At that point, she screamed.

Still transforming back to its native form, the creature effortlessly tossed Kyle's body aside as it twisted towards her. She tried to run for the exit, but the Bogeyman bounded on all-fours and grabbed her shin. There was a terrible crack of bones audible above the generator – as the creature twisted her leg off with a single yank. Anna was still screaming as she fell, blood rapidly pouring from the wound.

The Boogeyman threw the limb aside and turned to face Dillon.

She was trapped. The power lever was between them, but even if she shut it off, it would do nothing for her present situation other than turn the lights off and trap her in a dark room with a murderous Bogeyman.

It hunched like a gorilla on all-fours. Its transformation was complete. Covered in lank black hair, it blended into the shadows. Its enormous broad nose sniffed, savoring the hormonal cocktail of fear Dillon was now experiencing. All it would take was one lunge, and she was dead.

She pressed herself against the wall and shut her eyes tight.

She didn't see Elwood storm into the room. Or his

elation vanished when he saw the Bogeyman in his path, while slipping on the blood washing across the floor. He fell to his ass and rolled hard into the wall – accidentally firing his vapo.

The ion blast took a chunk out of the cinder block wall, dislodging the end of a steel roof joist. Concrete chunks fell down, narrowly missing Dillon. She darted forward, trying to dodge around the distracted Bogeyman – but it moved faster than she could. It pounced on her back – thrusting her to the ground. Its powerful jaws snapped down, breaking her neck.

Crumpled on the floor, Elwood could only watch in horror. He'd seen his share of blood in the field, but it never got any easier. He slid the vapo from under him and shot the Bogeyman.

The blast blew its head clean off. The body kicked and thrashed on top of Dillon, but she was already dead. The creature's bulk wasn't enough to absorb the ion stream. The shot smashed into the side of the transformer.

The pitch of the machinery became deafening. Elwood staggered to his feet. He no longer needed to power the substation down – it was about to explode.

"I know you can hear me, Sean!" Lisa was hoarse from yelling. "Come over here right now! Right this minute!"

Sean whimpered, clasping his hands tighter over his

ears. The Reaper remained poised over the children, unmoving.

"They can't!" Mike hissed. "It's got 'em good!"

"How did you break from it?" Wes asked, dragging his gaze away from the mass.

Mike tugged at his uniform, showing the basketball size tear in it. Wes could see the teeth marks in the flesh below.

"Something took a bite outta me. Brought me straight back to earth with a bump." If it wasn't for one nibbling phantom, the Welshman might have set all the timers early and freed the Reaper.

Lisa snarled. "You can't have my kids, you son-of-a-bitch."

She strode forward, fighting every instinct in her body. She reached out for her children. "Give me your hands!"

Then something shoved her from the side. She dropped to the floor. The burly Welshman had tackled her and was sprinting towards the kids with a war cry.

"Get your arses up!" he snapped, reaching for them. They resisted, desperate to get out of his reach.

"What're you doing?" Lisa screamed as he raised his open palm.

"Something good for once," Mike snarled. With his one good arm, he slapped both children hard across their cheeks. They flinched and burst into tears.

"NO!" Lisa screamed, crawling desperately towards them.

Both kids snapped around to see her and shouted, "Mom!"

Broken from their trance, they crawled towards her as the Reaper issued a canine-like howl and lashed at the energy screen.

Sparks popped and crackled as it put all its strength into

pushing a gnarled, clawed hand through the barrier. It only made it a foot out before the screen pulsed and the hand snapped back behind the screen. But it was enough to graze Mike's back.

The Angel of Death's touch carried with it a decaying force.

In less than a second, a patch of clothing on Mike's back became brittle and decomposed as the talon pushed into his skin. It was only the smallest of nicks before the paw was yanked back into the screen, but it was enough. A black necrotizing botch radiated across his body, decaying flesh in seconds, and working its way into his core.

Mike managed two steps before his entire body popped into a cloud of gray dust.

Sean and Emma ran into their mother's arms, and she held them tight, planting wild kisses on both of them.

Wes frantically wiped the Mike-dust off him and ran to join them.

"Let's get the hell out of here!"

They turned for the service door the children had entered through when the hissing static invaded their minds.

"Reeelleeassseee meeee…"

Lisa hesitated, but Wes roughly shoved her forward, hoping any physical jolt would focus away from the beast. As he passed the monitoring panel that the children had been originally sheltering behind, its voice became gentle.

"Looowweerrr the ssshield…"

Wes felt his hand reaching for the touch screen. He grabbed his wrist with his other hand and sank his fingernails into the exposed flesh. It was painful enough to snap his attention back to himself.

"FASTER!" he yelled at Lisa, although she was already sprinting down the corridor, herding the children ahead.

The Reaper howled and thrashed. Its tantrum threw sparks and across the screen, but it held. Wes couldn't believe they were going to get away with the rescue.

Lisa booted the door's crossbar, and it snapped open. Back outside, the intense heat seemed like a luxury compared to the humid Enclave. They even had to squint against the brightness of the SkyShield.

Wes stopped suddenly and looked up. That wasn't right.

The sky had taken on a bright pink hue as jagged electrical bolts arced from one wall to the other. Lisa stopped to watch.

"What's happening?"

The distinctive sound of an explosion drew their attention to the north, in time to see an orange fist of fire rise over the palm trees.

Then the SkyShield vanished.

"Oh my God..." Lisa moved closer to Wes. "Does that mean they can get out?"

Wes nodded mutely. One of his worst fears had just come to pass.

"E-everything?" asked Sean.

They all slowly turned back to the Enclave, acutely aware that they could no longer hear the Reaper's desperate wailing. Instead, there was dead silence.

They saw movement at the side of the pyramid where the trams entered. Without the SkyShield, darkness consumed everything. Yet there was an unmistakable shadow of something massive emerging from the Enclave.

The Angel of Death was free.

Chapter 24

The force of the exploding substation was directed straight up. A fiery orange punctuation mark was visible for miles around, although the shock wave was relatively small, taking the roofs off the surrounding maintenance hangars and shattering the few windows that hadn't already been destroyed. The carcass of the transformer was launched hundreds of feet, crashing down in the desert just beyond the west wall.

The moment the shield was down, the tens of thousands of guests who were still alive, broke from hiding and ran for their lives – straight into the massive blockade of emergency vehicles, press crews and curious gawkers who had gathered the moment the shield had gone up. It had already made international news. By the time the sound of the explosion rippled over the crowd and the shield had fallen, many of the reporters were broadcasting live in time to capture the pale, bloodied and harrowed horde of people running from the darkness like a horde of zombies.

Nobody stopped to take questions. Reporters and cops

were shouldered aside. Hundreds of injured people were intercepted by a fleet of ambulance crews, but even the injured didn't want to loiter any longer than they had to.

They knew what was behind them.

Phantoms didn't move quickly. They didn't have to. Although the survivors emerged from every direction when the SkyShield fell, they still funneled through the twenty gates to escape. The bottleneck provided ample opportunity for a few of the specters and higher class phantoms to cause carnage amongst the sitting ducks.

On the other side of the wall, the mass of people was further slowed by the huge crowds of spectators who had gathered. The phantoms themselves were no longer hindered by the wall, so flew over or phased through with impunity. Some took chunks out of the crowd as television cameras turned on the slavering creatures. A Fox News anchor was torn apart live on air, while a fleeing CNN reporter was crushed when a galloping wight headbutted the news van, rolling it over onto the terrified woman.

Wes and Lisa ran into the maintenance area, intending to make it to the command hub. Sean and Emma stuck close, neither saying a word. The cool desert air had bled away the furnace like atmosphere, giving them all a new lease of energy. Wes spotted a cluster of people around a maintenance hangar.

They glanced up as several helicopters soared low over-head. A police chopper cast its spotlight on the dark avenues, while several news choppers angled for the perfect shots.

"Blake!" He waved and ran over to see the group were clustered around Elwood, who was bleeding down the side of his face. He looked singed and angry. Blake quickly brought them up to speed.

"The Reaper's out," Wes said flatly.

Blake leaned back against a thirty-six-seater Ford bus, painting black and used to ferry staff between the park and city. He ran his hand through his hair and shook his head.

"That's it then…"

A chorus of sirens drew their attention as several police cars and ambulances drove through the delivery gate and zeroed towards the only people they could see. The next few minutes were taken up with paramedics tending to everybody's wounds. Elwood lay on a gurney, in the back on an ambulance as his superficial burns were treated, while Clarkson lay in another, hamming up his injuries. An unmarked black Escalade with a blue light on its dash skidded to a halt. A man jumped out, wearing shorts and a short-sleeved red shirt, looking exactly like a man who had been unwillingly plucked from a casino. Despite that, the cops treated him with respect as he flashed a badge at Blake.

"Mike Trent. I'm in charge of this mess… apparently."

Blake asked to see the badge again. "The Department? The Department of what?" He looked at the nearest cop, who shrugged.

"Homeland Security says he's in charge," the cop said, as if it explained everything.

"We have jurisdiction over the pan creatures," Trent mumbled by way of explanation. He was clearly out of his depth. "The new exhibit, this Reaper. Just how bad is it?"

Wes and Blake exchanged a looked. "You mean the Angel of Death? The clue is in the title," Blake said. He was too exhausted for bullshit.

Trent rubbed his hand over his mouth. He was still coming to terms with what was unfolding.

"It was seen heading north."

"It's drawn to the people there," said Wes. "Like a moth to a light."

Trent nodded. "Thing is, all the other ghosts and things were trailing behind it. Like the Pied Piper. Straight to the city. I thought these were supposed to be wild animals? I've seen the show." He gave a little smile and wave to Elwood in the back of the ambulance opposite. "Big fan. So, why are they suddenly grouping together?"

Sean suddenly spoke up.

"It's gathering an army."

Elwood snorted dismissively. "Shut up, kid. You don't know what you're talking about."

Sean's eyes narrowed. "You know what, Mister Elwood. I think I know more than you. At least one of us read your book."

Despite the tension, Wes couldn't hold back a snickering laugh.

Sean wasn't finished. "I heard it talking to me." He tapped his head. "It wanted freedom. It wanted control. It can communicate telepathically with the other phantoms." He caught Elwood's look. "It's on page twenty-five. Y'know, you used to be my hero."

"Heroes don't die, kid. I still am." Elwood forced his trademark grin, now that all the police officers were looking at him.

"No. You're a disappointment. When Em and I needed somebody, we had our mom." Lisa couldn't hold back a sob. "And we had Wes."

Wes burned with embarrassment as everybody looked at him.

"He's right," said Blake. "On all counts." He shot Elwood a disappoint look. "We've given it an army."

"How do we stop it?" Trent's question was met with flat silent. He turned to Elwood. "You've done it before."

"That was when it was on its own, and there was a team of us." Elwood gestured to his injuries. "And I wasn't falling apart."

Wes gave him a black look, sure that Elwood was playing up his injuries to hide his cowardice.

Trent looked desperately at them all. "There were sixty thousand people trapped in here." He stabbed a finger towards the ground. "And if you think what just happened was bad, then remember there are two-point-five million in Vegas. And that's without the extra million visitors there probably are right now."

Vegas didn't need walls. The desert made it an open prison. There was nowhere to go, and very few places to hide.

Blake spoke his thoughts aloud. "Maybe if we can take the big guy down, the others will apport or disperse. Make it easier for the hunting teams to mop them up." He didn't see the need to add that the hunting teams were currently deployed around the world and couldn't make it back for days. "The only issue is that he's the only one who's done it," he indicated to Elwood. "We don't have the people-power."

"But we have that." Wes pointing to the armor-plated Oshkosh L-ATV parked at the back of the parade convoy. The ten-thousand-pound beast was the Army's replacement for the faithful Humvee. This one had been painted in the park's livery, complete with Phamo giving the thumbs up on the door. An eight-foot-long Vaporizer was mounted on a rear gimbal.

Blake looked doubtful. "The Beast is a prototype."

"But does it work?" Trent prompted.

"The vapo has a one point eight-terawatt Ion stream. It'll bring our Angel of Death to its proverbial knees. Unfortunately, the range is only about five yards, then the stream is too weak."

"That's not close," said Wes. "That's intimate."

"It's a suicide run!" snarked Elwood.

"It's all we've got," Blake said flatly.

Trent clapped his hands in what he hoped was a motivational way. "Come on, Mister Elwood. We're counting on you."

Elwood clambered from the back of the ambulance, wincing with each step as he approached the vehicle. He sized it up. Then shook his head. "I'm in no state to go."

Blake leaned into him, lowering his voice so as not to embarrass Elwood. "I don't give a crap about your undistinguished career record. As far as I'm concerned, it never left the hub. But I'm in charge of this park and you're going to do this."

Elwood lowered his voice to match Blakes. "I can't." He looked away, chagrinned.

"I'll do it."

Blake looked dismissively at Wes. "No offence Wes, but you don't have the training this guy has. No matter what he thinks."

"You know what, Blake. I always blamed Calvin for not promoting me. But you could have overridden his decision any time, but I suppose you were in the throes of hero-worship and listening to him." He patted Elwood on the shoulder. "An asshole who never got my name right. Even when it was on my nametag."

Elwood nodded somberly. "West is right. I could never remember it. Besides, he's the one who went out there tonight. I think there's a better man." He placed a hand on Wes's shoulder in solidarity.

Wes gave a tight smile. "Thanks for that. Of course, you're only saying that because it gets you off the hook." He shucked Elwood's hand away and opened the Oshkosh's door.

Inside, an iPad had been gaffer taped to the dash, with wires running from it, bunching into a box of electronics taped to the floor. Blake opened the other door and leaned in. The iPad came to life, and he opened an app. It showed a video feed from the giant vapo.

"This is simple point and shoot tech." He traced a finger across the screen. With a whirl of servos, the enormous weapon swung around to trace his movements. His finger hovered over a red button. "And fire with this. You only have two charges. Well, in theory. So make the first one count."

Wes' mouth was too dry to comment. Lisa leaned against him, her hand gently rubbing his back.

"Are you sure you know what you're doing?"

"When has that ever stopped me?"

Her hand ran up his cheek, drawing him closer. "Be careful, Wes." She suddenly kissed him. It was soft, passionate, and unexpected. She slowly pulled away, resting her forehead against his. "We need you back. We've got a lot to discuss." She pecked him on the lips, then returned to her children – both of whom were smirking.

Wes threw his vapo onto the passenger seat. He was about to climb in, but stopped and crossed over to Trent and Elwood.

"If I'm doing this, then you're doing something for me." He pointed to the bus. "Take Lisa and the kids, and anybody else who wants to, out of this city. Now."

Trent nodded. "Sure thing."

"I can do that," Elwood said with conviction. Wes pulled Elwood's vapo off his shoulder.

"I'm sure you can. Get them as far as possible" He crossed to Sean and handed him the vapo. Sean took it reverently.

"Wow! Can I come with you?"

Wes crouched to be level with him. "No. You have something just as important to do. Look after your mom and sister." He stole a glance at Elwood, who was climbing into the bus's driving seat. "He can't do it. He needs a real hero."

Sean gave a solemn nod. "I can do that."

Emma suddenly threw her arms around him and squeezed him tight. "Come back soon, Wes!"

He could barely keep the tears away. Lisa wasn't able to.

"I will, Em."

Without a further word, he climbed into the Oshkosh and turned the three-hundred forty horsepower engine over. It growled fiercely. He watched as Elwood beeped his horn, motioning for Lisa and the kids to climb aboard. Clarkson hobbled aboard, ushering his paramedics away.

Wes pulled from the shed and was joined by a pair of police cars running their lights and sirens to clear his way. Within moments, he was through the gates and speeding along the freeway towards the beckoning lights of Downtown Vegas.

Chapter 25

Vegas was too much of a lure. The blistering light show of the Strip combined with the concentrated mass of humanity was everything the phantoms sought when they slipped into our world. Even at 4am, the city was more alive than any other, crammed with people oblivious to the catastrophic events a few miles to the south.

A stretch limo, filled with six drunk women sucking every last molecule of joy from their bachelorette party, were singing to Taylor Swift's *Look at What You Made Me Do* as the driver pulled out from Park Avenue, next to the *New York-New York Hotel*. Something broadsided them at speed. Gunk splashed over the side windows, causing the passengers to scream. Fearing he'd struck somebody, the driver shifted into park and got out. Sunroofs slid back, and the women peered out, phones at the ready.

The side of the limo was covered in slime that throbbed and pulsed as it reconstituted towards the middle of the mass. The driver had seconds to ponder what was happening – when a wailing specter swooped down and plucked him into the air.

The bachelorettes fell into mute shock as they tracked his kicking body as it was lifted over the hotel's roller coaster before he was dropped. His screams stopped when he landed headfirst on the track, then spun off and crumbled on the concrete floor.

With a glutinous sucking noise, the ectoplasm on the side of the car formed back into the grotesque phantom that had struck the vehicle. Powerful jaws bit down on one woman's camera, slicing the hand off at the wrist. She convulsed in silent shock as the others screamed and dropped back into the limo for cover.

The phantom phased into the car. It violently rocked on its suspension as the creature carved its way through the occupants like a blender. Blood smattered the windshield, and the vehicle was knocked out of park. It rolled into the boulevard – where it was broadsided by a speeding Mack truck. The women were dead before the limo buckled in half.

It was the first sign of the terror to come.

A troupe of Elvis impersonators hauled their guitar cases to the trunk of their replica Cadillac Eldorado, which was idling outside the curved undulations of Planet Hollywood. The gig had gone fine. As a tribute act, there was little that could go wrong, and now they wanted nothing more than head to their homes and sleep.

Screams made them all look towards the entrance to the Miracle Mile shops. Even at this late hour, the escalators were filled with people hitching a ride up to the bridge, crossing the boulevard. All eyes were on the thirty-foot figure stomping towards them. A massive humanoid dressed in ancient Egyptian robes. Arms the size of tree trunks lashed out at the vehicles skidding around its feet. Its head was that of a ferocious jackal, its skin as dark as ebony. The Reaper had taken the form of Anubis, the ancient Egyptian God of death. It was the same guise it had worn when Elwood had faced it in Egypt, and the one it had settled on as it passed the Luxor Hotel further down the strip.

It clubbed together its massive fists and swung them down on the bridge. Concrete and metal buckled as it decayed and corroded. People caught in the crush erupted into clouds of ash. The Reaper roared as it pushed the rapidly dissolving bridge aside. The asphalt under its feet bubbled and disintegrated, leaving gigantic footprints in its wake.

The Elvises watched in shock as it kicked aside a taxi. By the time the cab smashed through the glass façade of the Cosmopolitan, it was already a rusted hulk. The Reaper's foot came crashing down, flattening the Cadillac. Two of the Elvises burst into ash. The remaining two turned and ran. They made it ten yards before a pack of phantoms bore down on them. More followed, filling the boulevard with terror.

Wes mashed the gas pedal to the floor, maxing out the Oshkosh at seventy. The traffic was building ahead, but parted as two police cars guiding him up the I15. They looped off the freeway and onto Tropicana. Wes followed close. They seemed to know exactly where to go. Traffic on the opposite side was getting heavier as people tried to flee the city.

Only when he reached the corner of South Las Vegas did he get an inkling of what lay ahead. The Statue of Liberty on the corner of the New York-New York hotel had toppled into the street, crushing cars and forcing others to deviate around it. A cordon of armed police vehicles blocked access to the Strip, with frantically waving officers were detouring traffic. They parted as the cruisers approached. One driver leaned out of his window and motioned for Wes to continue. The officers ahead pulled back the barriers.

"Don't think," muttered Wes. "Just do."

He overtook the cruisers and turned northbound onto the boulevard – and straight into a nightmare. The bridge between the New York-New York and the MGM had collapsed. Both hotels were in darkness, and he could see flames licking the side of the MGM. Dozens of vehicles - cabs, cars, trucks – were abandoned in the road, many on their sides and heavily corroded under the Reaper's touch. More were aflame. The absence of bodies was a false blessing when he noticed the breeze kicking up plumes of gray ash.

The engine growled as he picked up speed again, passing the Hard Rock Cafe with the neck of its iconic giant guitar snapped off. A few phantoms dodged in and out of the broken windows. He glimpsed people cowering or throwing chairs at them as they were attacked.

He suddenly slammed on the brakes as a group of people cut across his path. The Oshkosh skidded, slewing sideways – but didn't stop in time to avoid a herd of wights galloping from the branching Mosaic access road.

One slammed into the fender, exploding in a mass of

ectoplasm that smothered the windshield. The beast reformed behind the vehicle, snorted irritably at him, then continued to pursue its drunk quarry. Wes looked at the raft of switches on the dash, thumbing every one until the wipers suddenly grated across the gloop, smearing it until it became worse.

Then he crashed into the side of a wagon. He would have gone straight through the windshield if the seat restraint hadn't held him firmly in place. He unbuckled the harness, opened the door, and used the sill to stand on so he could lean out and wipe the crap off the window with his sleeve. He had clipped the edge of a mobile billboard sporting a huge advertisement for live strippers. The stylish angled Dolce & Gabbana building across the street was smashed up and on fire. Screams and gunshots came from every direction.

Ahead, a score of phantoms flocked in a spiral over the boulevard, before dive-bombing a target that was out of view. A handful of people across the street fled for their lives, some covered in the ash of the dead, others bleeding and barely able to walk. Glitching digital billboards added to the bizarreness of the scene.

At the intersection ahead, a police cruiser had collided with a pickup. The cops were out and shooting at two phantoms bobbing and weaving overhead. Two Hispanic guys, covered in tattoos and armed with automatic weapons, crawled from the pickup. Dazed, they joined the cops in repelling the spooks, but even the onslaught of automatic gunfire simply passed through them.

Enraged, Wes snatched his vapo from the passenger seat. Hopping down from the armored vehicle, he pumped the weapon alive.

"Hey! Ecto-breath!" The phantoms snarled when they

spotted him. There was a glimmer of recognition. "Get the hell out of my dimension."

He unleashed an ion stream. The phantoms tried to jink aside but were struck. They dropped to the road like wet sacks. Irate, they tried to crawl away. The hollering hoods and cops rounded on them, emptying everything they had into the critters. The phantoms exploded across the intersection in a puddle of bubbling mucus.

Cops and gangsters gave each other a high-five, and for a moment Wes was taken by the rare display of humanity bonding.

Then the ectoplasm flowed as they began to reform. Gnarled fingers emerged from the puddle.

"No fair!" howled one gangbanger, squeezing his trigger. His clip was dry.

"Water!" Wes looked around. "We need water!" He spotted a fire hydrant on the corner and remembered the poltergeist. The cop followed his gaze and understood. He jumped into the cruiser and reversed. Metal grated as the vehicles came free from one another. The two hoods stomped the phantoms' reforming arms.

With a whoop from the siren, the cop sped straight into the hydrant and skidded to a stop. Water erupted at high pressure, bucking the car, which deflected it across the junction. The moment it came in contact with the ectoplasm, it diluted it, washing it away and leaving four malformed arms flapping like fish. The cops and gangsters once again cheered.

Wes' moment of triumph was extinguished when something exploded further up the boulevard, followed by a bellow of terror which was punctuated by a loud roar which he instantly recognized.

He'd found the Reaper.

Chapter 26

Tobias Elwood was lost in deep thought as he drove the bus. He was following the vehicle's sat nav, which Lisa had used to find her address. She wanted to get the kids some fresh clothes from home before leaving town, and Elwood has taken up the role of chauffer without complaint.

He glanced in the mirror and saw Lisa was curled up on a seat with Emma. They were both fast asleep. Sean sat at the back, stifling a yawn as he examined the vapo. Elwood's eyes darted to Lisa, wondering what a woman like her saw in Wes. He gave a low chuckle, pleased that he'd finally remembered his name.

Not that he disliked Wes. Back before he was famous, he could have tolerated the guy as a friend. It was the fame that had changed Elwood. His rise in popularity, and the accompanying fortune that rolled in, had narrowed his perception of other people. All his life, he'd struggled to hold on to a job. And relationships were a no-go. Sure, he got the cream of vacuous models, but there was nothing substantial or interesting about them. After a week, he would grow bored and have to move on.

Only now did he realize that was exactly what they were thinking, too.

He was a celebrity. A one-trick pony. And like all tricks, his personality was an illusion.

Now he thought about it, that was what he had found irritating about Wes. He was smart, interesting and likable. When you're a handsome A-lister, that warranted a triple-threat.

He blindly followed the sat nav as he was yet again diverted. He flinched as four LVMPD SWAT vans roared past, lights blazing. It drew Sean's attention. He put the vapo down and walked to the front.

"Where are we?"

"Don't you know you're not supposed to distract the driver?" He was still smarting from the kid's public burn, even if everything he had said rang true.

Sean pointed over the roofs of the low buildings around them. Several helicopters soared across the city, searchlights playing on the streets below. "Are they going to the Strip?"

"Of course not," said Elwood. "Your mom said you lived way on the other side, or we wouldn't be going there. Sit back down. Let me concentrate."

He heard Lisa stir, woken up by the conversation.

"Where are we?" she said between yawns.

Elwood swung a left as the sat nav diverted them once again. Lisa suddenly appeared at his shoulder, looking around in concern.

"Elwood… what're you doing?"

"This thing's got me rolling around in circles."

"We're on the wrong side of town," she said urgently.

Elwood sighed. "Great! I was following this thing. Are you're saying I've got us lost?"

"No. I'm saying you've got us killed."

Thousands of people flooded across South Las Vegas Boulevard as they fled from the slaughter. Flames licked from the upper floors of the Bellagio as a swarm of Phantoms phased in and out of the rooms like a locust plague. Across the street, the casinos of the Paris were being ransacked by more phantoms, specters, and a pair of Bogeymen that had infiltrated a restaurant. But the main source of their terror came from the giant Anubis, clinging to the foot of the Eiffel Tower.

Helicopters noisily circled around it, catching it with their spotlights. Most were news crews broadcasting the disaster live around the world. Two police choppers had marksmen hanging from the side doors, taking pointless shots at the beast.

A pair of Apache AH-64E attack helicopters from the nearby Nellis Air Force Base roared low over the boulevard. Their M230 chain guns unleashed a barrage of gunfire – which passed harmlessly through the Reaper. Chunks were torn from the tower and the metal corroded under the phantom's touch. With a mighty rending of twisted metal - the structure toppled across the boulevard.

The Reaper hopped to the ground as the tower smashed through one of the Apaches, which exploded, and it was forced down into Bellagio's pool with a colossal splash. Fiery debris rained down across the street.

The second gunship bobbed aside – then unleashed its complement of AGM-114 Hellfire missiles straight at the Angel of Death. They passed straight through it and struck the tower block of the Paris hotel, demolishing it.

The crew barely had time to register their shock. A phantom the size of a sofa suddenly flew in front of them, blocking their view. The chain gun spun to track it – but it moved too fast as it darted *into* the cockpit.

The pilots never had a chance. The chopper spun around, banking sharply as it lost altitude and crashed into the lower stories of Caesar's Palace. The explosion shook the building, taking out all the windows. A fraction of a second later, the gunship's remaining ammunition cooked, causing a further massive explosion–

The entire Caesar's Palace tower collapsed down on itself as it lost all structural integrity. A huge black and gray cloud billowed over the Bellagio and Paris. The circling helicopters were forced to gain altitude to avoid it. Anybody caught on the ground was suddenly left gasping for breath, convinced they had entered hell.

The Reaper howled at the sky as it absorbed the collective fear. It swelled another ten foot in size. Never had it felt so powerful as it marshaled the lowly phantoms around it. Telepathically connected, it sensed something was wrong. It turned to trace the cause of the disturbance...

Wes didn't dare got above thirty as he sped towards the rolling dust cloud. He was too afraid of running anybody over, as yet more people fled for their lives. Packs of phantom swooped in pursuit, driven by a combination of newfound bloodlust and the Angel of Death goading them on.

He kept one hand on the wheel, the other was holding the heavy vapo out of the side window. The hood took most of the weight as he randomly blasted at the phantoms in his path. Every time he got one, it would shriek as it solidified and dropped to the floor – where he would runover it seconds later.

The Reaper turned and hissed at him. It crouched, ready to attack. Wes hit the iPad screen and powered up the Vaporizer. He had to get close, and at that moment, he was certain this was a one-way trip. It always had been. The fleeting fantasies about getting together with Lisa that he'd harbored on the drive in had kept him going. But he understood they were *just* fantasies. Elwood may have captured the Angel of Death, but Wes would go down in history as the man who killed it.

The vapo's display beeped an acknowledgement that it was fully charged. The gun-camera had the beast right in his sights. He tried to ignore Blake's words that this was an untested prototype. It had to work.

All he had to do was close the gap.

Wes floored the gas.

The Oshkosh spurred forward.

Wes swore the Anubis recognized him. Its face contorted in a snarl, and it ran to intercept him.

The Oshkosh touched on fifty – seconds from slamming through the beast. Wes triggered the vapo and pushed himself back in his seat to brace for the impact.

The searing Ion stream shot overhead with such ferocity, the metal on the cab's roof bubbled. It hit the Reaper in the chest. Jagged electrical streamers coursed over its body – dephasing it as it became solid - just as the vehicle impacted into it.

The world suddenly became a whirling maelstrom.

Wes was thrown in his seat – held in place by the harness – as the ten-thousand-pound vehicle flipped over. The vapo bounced around the cab, forcing him to cover his head with both arms. It struck him hard several times. With a deafening crunch, the windshield shattered, and the Oshkosh slid along the road, upside down, before coming to a halt.

Wes couldn't believe he was still alive. He braced himself for a further attack, but nothing came. Had he killed the Angel of Death? He laughed, hysterical and relieved.

Then he heard the hissing. It took him several seconds to locate the source.

The front of the vehicle was rapidly turning black as a wave of corrosion edged towards him. Now he knew what he was looking at, he could just make out the crumpled form of the Anubis lying across his path. It was now so big that it filled his field of view. Dead or alive, its decaying touch was still lethal.

The decay was midway across the hood and advancing. Wes struggled to unlock his harness. The latches were tight; it hadn't been designed to easily release while inverted, and his own body weight was trapping him.

He became frantic as the field of decay spread to the dashboard. Metal, glass and plastic turned to dust. Fragments fell from the floor *above* him as that dissolved, too.

With a desperate bellow, he unclipped one harness. It was enough to tip him sideways from the seat – just as the bolts holding the seat in place corroded and the heavy chair dropped to the ceiling, narrowly missing his head.

Wes shouldered the passenger door open. It fell from rusting hinges, and he crawled out. He reached for the vapo inside – but pulled his hand back as the front half of the vehicle dissolved into a pile of dust. The weapon disintegrated before his very eyes.

He pushed himself further away. The giant Anubis lay motionless against the wall of the Bellagio Fountain pool. Its chest had caved in from where the Oshkosh had collided with its solid form. Bile and ectoplasm oozed out, smelling like strong vomit.

Wes couldn't summon the energy to be triumphant. He was beyond exhausted. He stared at his vanquished opponent.

"That's what you get for messing up my dimension." Every word hurt his ribs.

The Anubis's eye flicked open. Its double pupils, each the size of a plate, contracted as it focused on him. A strangled cry caught in Wes' throat. He flipped over and crawled away. Every time he tried to stand his legs buckled beneath him.

The crumbling Oshkosh was battered aside. It rolled twice before breaking into rusting dust. Wes could hear the Reaper's labored breathing; it was hurt. Blue blood and ectoplasm oozed from its stomach wound as it lashed a huge palm at him – just missing. The road surface beneath hissed and dissolve.

Wes tried to stand again, but couldn't. He fell flat, rolling onto his back in time to see the Reaper push itself up on its knees. One hand rubbed the gaping hole in its chest, examining the wound with curiosity.

The surrounding smoke and dust were tinged red from the fires. Wes dropped flat on his back, every ounce of strength depleted. He watched as the cloud above swirled, and then a news chopper bravely descended through the smoke. The cameraman leaning from the door, capturing Wes' final moments.

This is how it was going to end for him. Killed on live TV. Fame at last.

The camera suddenly shifted off him. The enormous jackal head snapped up, looking beyond Wes. He was too tired to turn. The Reaper tried to climb to its feet. There was a blur as something roared past him so close that he could feel the breeze. A long black vehicle. He caught the hint of a cartoon ghost on the fender – before it slammed into the Reaper at speed.

Now solidified, the Reaper couldn't avoid the Phantom Land bus striking it at speed. Elwood was at the wheel, bellowing with fury. Momentum staggered the creature back as its flesh tore, pouring more ectoplasm over the vehicle. It teetered into the Bellagio Fountains. A second later, the bus struck the fountain wall and was ramped into the air.

The bus twisted sideways, landing on top of the Anubis, pinning it in the pool. It thrashed as water reacted with the ectoplasm. Drained of all its strength, it couldn't push the vehicle aside. The news chopper moved closer, capturing every moment as the beast dissolved in the pool, leaving nothing more than an oily residue on the surface of the water. Tobias Elwood clambered from a broken window and stood on top of the vehicle.

"Time to fry, sucker!"

Wes didn't hear. He was fading in and out of consciousness.

Chapter 27

The moment Tobias Elwood slayed the Angel of Death by bravely driving a bus into it, was broadcast live around the world. As was the moment that he heroically scooped Wes up and carried him towards a fleet of approaching emergency vehicles. The footage was always looped just before Wes woke up, struggled from his arms, and started arguing with Elwood.

Most of the other pans had apported back to their own dimension the moment they were released from the Reaper's commanding presence. A few had gone into hiding and would be later rooted out by hunting teams.

Sitting on the tailgate of an ambulance, Wes allowed a paramedic to clean his wounds. His arm was broken and hanging in a sling, but with more serious mass injuries, his were at the back of the cue. Vegas's entire emergency services had arrived in a wall of police cars, ambulances and fire trucks, further assisted by just about everything they had at Nellis Air Force Base.

Every news team in the area was descending on the ambulance and the hero that had saved the day.

Tobias Elwood.

Wes winced as an antiseptic wipe dabbed his face. Lisa watched with a half-smile. Since getting lost, Elwood had circled back and inadvertently cut across the Strip as he blindly followed the sat nav. It had been Sean who had spotted Wes's gallant charge in the Oshkosh. Elwood had slammed on the brakes, and in an uncharacteristic moment of guilt, spun the bus in a wide turn, intending to help. He'd ordered Lisa and the kids off. At the time, she'd argued that throwing them to the mercies of the phantoms was suicidal – until she understood his half-baked plan.

And that was all the world had seen. Elwood was the hero of the day.

Lisa draped her arms around Wes, and they fell into a long, lazy kiss.

"The world should know who the real hero is," she whispered.

They watched as the press swamped Elwood just yards away. Not a single camera turned in their direction. Elwood was back to his old self, oozing charm and confidence to enraptured reporters.

Wes gave a resigned sigh. "I don't think anybody cares."

"I care."

She kissed him again, and all he could feel was a stinging pain shooting through his face. He was seriously thinking that a higher power had it in for him.

"Mister Talasky." He looked up to see Mike Trent approaching. He glanced around the destruction with the expression of one who had seen it all before. "That was quite a stunt you guys pulled off."

He paused, waiting for Wes to fill in the conversation. When he didn't, Trent continued, uneasily.

"Um, so I work for an International Government organization who deals in situations like this." He gestured to the burning Bellagio Hotel and the mound of rubble that was once Caesar's Palace.

"I don't imagine you get many of them," Lisa said.

Trent gave a dry chuckle. "Oh, you'd be surprised." He fixed his gaze back on Wes. "We're always looking for people with expertise in *unusual* areas."

Wes glanced at Lisa. Despite everything, he was intrigued. His commitment to the Park had ended the moment he had woken up in Elwood's arms. An experience made worse by the fact it was now viral across social media. Sean had showed him the live stream on Lisa's cell phone, which had survived everything with just a single fracture across the screen. To save Wes's embarrassment, she had sent the kids to sit on the fender of a SWAT van. Wes still had bills to pay and was open to new opportunities.

Trent gestured around. "And this certainly qualifies as unusual. So I was wondering," he moved closer. "Do you think Elwood would be interested in leaving the park and joining us?"

Wes treated him to a lizard-like blink. With a groan, he stood up and drew closer to Trent.

"I don't know. You'd have to talk to his agent. And I hear she's real nasty." He nodded to the surrounding wreckage. "Worse than this."

He draped his good arm around Lisa, and he limped away with as much dignity as he could muster. His answer appeared to have thrown Trent.

"Oh. Thanks. Hey, if we need to talk to you, can we find you at the park?"

Wes stopped and threw him a look. "I don't work there anymore. If you need me, I'll be around."

They marshaled Sean and Emma together and slowly headed westwards towards their homes, just as dawn was breaking.

Emma tugged at Lisa's arm.

"Next Halloween, can we go to Disney World? All four of us?"

Wes looked into Lisa's eyes, and for the first time saw hope. And a future.

He ruffled Emma's hair. "Sure. Why not? What's the worst that could happen there?"

Also by Andy Briggs

EPICENTER

Majestic Files 1

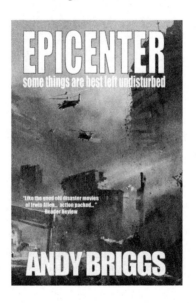

SOME THINGS ARE BEST LEFT UNDISTURBED...

An **earthquake** strikes - and with it several bizarre murders.

Something is emerging from beneath the earth – leaving behind destruction and carnage.

A terrible **secret** has been disturbed.

And now it's poised to trigger a disaster that will **destroy** the world...

CHEM

Majestic Files 2

Not all conspiracy theories are wrong…

Aircraft vapor trails slice through the skies around the world. A harmless side effect to international travel. Until aircraft investigator Sam Dwyer discovers something bolted to the wing of a fatal crash. Something that shouldn't be there…

He stumbles into a global conspiracy to lace the skies with chemtrails – chemicals designed to alter the population's behavior. It's an intricate plot with global ramifications – and it's happening in plain sight!

With his life on the line, Dwyer races to expose the syndicate behind it. But their resources are vast. There is nowhere to hide…

POINT NEMO

Majestic Files 4

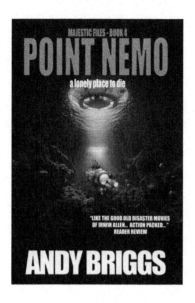

A LONELY PLACE TO DIE...

Point Nemo - the most **remote location** on the planet…

Deep below the waves it's known as the **satellite graveyard**…

…And something **terrifying is stirring**…

A group of scientists have been gathered to investigate a mysterious find. A threat that may not be from this world. A threat that could destroy life as we know it…

Now the world's superpowers are descending on Point Nemo in a race to claim it as their own.

A rip-roaring adventure!

Printed in Great Britain
by Amazon